Home Run Rudy

and His
Tattletale Teeth

Janet Garman

ChariotVICTOR
PUBLISHING
A DIVISION OF COOK COMMUNICATIONS

Chariot Books is an imprint of ChariotVictor Publishing
Cook Communications, Colorado Springs, CO 80918
Cook Communications, Paris, Ontario
Kingsway Communications, Eastbourne, England

HOME RUN RUDY AND HIS TATTLETALE TEETH

Designed by Andrea Boven
Cover illustration by Rick Johnson
First printing, 1998
Printed in United States of America

ISBN 0-78143-017-8
02 01 00 99 98   5 4 3 2 1

Library of Congress Cataloging-in-Publication Data

Garman, Janet.
        Home Run Rudy and his tattletale teeth / Janet Garman.
                p.   cm. -- (Home Run Rudy ; 1)
        Summary: Already known as the class clown, Rudy Benson gets in even more
trouble when his braces start picking up radio signals, allowing him to listen to the
World Series during class.
        ISBN 0-7814-3017-8
        [1. Schools--Fiction. 2. Christian life--Fiction.] I. Title. II. Series: Garman,
Janet. Home Run Rudy ; 1.
PZ7.G184156Ho   1998
[Fic]--DC21

                                                                                97-35522
                                                                                CIP
                                                                                AC

Dedication

To my husband, Paul, for his involvement and encouragement, and to the members of All Write Away, for their tireless critiques and helpful advice. God Bless you all!

Chapter

I

"Rudy? *Rudy Benson*! I asked you a question."

Ms. Throckmeir's mouth twisted as though she'd sucked a lemon. She clawed a strand of black hair out of her face and banged her pointer against the chalkboard.

"Sorry, Ms. Throck . . . My ears aren't too good this afternoon," Rudy croaked. Who could hear over the chanting of the fans?

Some of the girls tittered and Gwenny pressed her palms against her heart and whisper-sang: "Take me out to the ball game. . . . "

Not one boy moved a muscle. They sat as still as statues while Ms. Throckmeir strode over to Rudy's desk and lifted the red-headed twelve-year-old boy by the collar of his windbreaker.

Crack! Out fell his GPX radio, ripping loose from the wires as it hit the floor.

"*Martinez swings . . . the count is three and two, bases are loaded . . . a hit!*"

Ms. Throckmeir made a rude noise with her lips as she jabbed the off switch.

The sixth-grade boys let out a collective sigh. Ninth inning . . . the final play-off game . . . and now Rudy couldn't feed them the play-by-play.

Ms. Throckmeir's eyes bulged. "All you ever think about is baseball," she shouted. "After-school conference. You. Your parents. The principal."

Rudy tuned out. He noticed a thin string of spittle trickling from the left corner of Ms. Throckmeir's mouth. It swung back and forth as her face contorted.

He sighed. She was probably still uptight about the superintendent's visit during social studies yesterday. Rudy's group project was to create a relief map of Wyoming. It wasn't his fault Charlie Freeman's salt dough mountains accidentally formed themselves into an unflattering model of Ms. Throckmeir's face. Or that Morton Fleever added a wart on the end of her nose.

Ms. Throckmeir and the superintendent had spotted it at the same time. Her face blanched cauliflower white, but Dr. Yasuzawa's face burned bright red. The noise level was pretty high, what with Charlie's braying laughter and everybody working with partners, but Rudy knew from the superintendent's jabbing fists and a few words like "no discipline" and "need to demand quality work" that Ms. Throckmeir was in trouble.

He wasn't fooled later when she lectured the class

on "working quietly and productively with your group" and announced that Dr. Yasuzawa planned to "pop in" every few days to see how things were going.

At recess, Rudy hunkered down in a corner of the playground under the cottonwood tree with his best friends, Charlie Freeman and Morton Fleever. Instantly, they were surrounded by half the class— mostly Seventh Street Sluggers, the baseball team Rudy had organized last summer. They'd shot to stardom with a 44–14 record and dubbed him "Home Run Rudy" for obvious reasons.

Kevin Jorgenson moaned like a sick cow and collapsed on the sand.

"Whoooo-ee!" Morton drew the sound out like a long string of bubble gum. Everything about him from his nose to his grasshopper legs stuck out long and thin. "What'll we do now?"

"Skip school?" suggested Rusty.

"Stop fooling around. This is serious business," Rudy said.

"I'd bring my brother's pocket radio Monday," said Tony Perez. "But he'll need it himself, first day of the Series."

"Hey, Charlie," said Eddie. "How's the purse?"

Charlie's grin lit his dark brown face and his black eyes sparkled behind owl glasses as he patted his hip pocket.

"More'n eight dollars in here. Maybe nine, if

Rudy'd cough up." Charlie, a whiz kid in math, cele-
brated every sports event with wagers. He and Rudy
had been as tight as an Oreo cookie since kindergarten and usually thought alike. But ever since
Rudy's family had joined First Street Church in June,
Rudy stashed all his earnings for the youth group's
Thanksgiving camping trip with Dr. Mac. He'd saved
his money like he hoarded his best baseball cards,
but Charlie was as dense as a catcher's mitt about it.
Now, Charlie's constant badgering irritated him like
a mosquito bite.

"I told you I'm not gambling anymore because it's
a stupid waste of money."

Charlie pressed his hands together as if in prayer
and sang, "Money is the root of all ee-vil. Money is
the root of all ee-vil. Money. . ."

Rudy felt his face go hot. "The Bible says it's the
love of money that gets us into trouble, Money Man!"
he snapped. "I have better things to do with my
allowance than to blow it on your stupid football
pool."

"Cut it out, Charlie," Eddie said. Kevin and I
didn't ante up either, but look how much you got
without us."

Charlie shrugged and turned his back.

Rudy sat glumly picking a strand of bacon out of
his metal braces. Most of the boys had brought their
baseball cards, but no one felt like trading. Nobody
challenged him on game statistics either. Monday

was the Series. And they were going to miss it.

*   *   *   *   *

When the last school bus pulled away, Rudy braced himself. The school secretary waved him to the back office. Mr. Alvarez, the principal, hunched at one end of a long table, rubbing his mustache, which clung to his upper lip like a ragged eyebrow. Ms. Throckmeir sat stiffly at the other end. Rudy's parents perched together on the far side of the table. His dad sweated in a heavy, gray suit. Mom still wore her white, satin jacket with "Brenda Benson's Catering" embroidered on the front.

Rudy slid into the vacant seat facing her.

Most of the conference went exactly as Rudy had expected once Ms. Throckmeir displayed the radio, its cord still gloppy with Mom's Cover-All makeup. Allowance suspended indefinitely. Homework every afternoon as soon as he hit the house. A note to Rudy's parents every day from Ms. Throckmeir, reporting his behavior.

"Rudy has a lot of potential," Mr. Alvarez said, grimly. "But his attention is limited to baseball statistics, projecting the arc of a curve ball, and the physics involved in hitting a home run. We cannot design our academic program around baseball."

He shuffled through Rudy's file folder. "As you know, he was in the office more than thirty times last

year—including twenty-two times for silly and dis-
ruptive behavior in class, three times for upstaging
the speaker during an assembly, and once . . . ahem . . .
for hanging me in effigy on April Fool's Day."

Rudy faded out briefly. The usual stuff. He was
home safe. Then an inside slider nailed him, and he
blinked in shock.

"According to his placement tests from last
month, Rudy started sixth grade at least a year
behind in all subjects. Given his poor work habits, it
may be too late for him to catch up. He might need to
repeat sixth grade instead of going on to middle
school next year."

Alarm bells clanged in Rudy's head. *Not go on
with his friends? Left back with the little kids?* His breath
caught in his throat, and when he looked down, he
saw his T-shirt twitching right over his heart. He'd
lose his friends. He already was a head taller than
most of the kids in sixth. With his flyaway red hair,
he'd stand out like some humongous zit.

"Okay. Okay," he said, not recognizing the
squeaky sound of his own voice. "I'll do every single
assignment. Twice, if you want. I'll even bring our
tape recorder and record everything Ms. Throckmeir
says. And I'll listen to the tape at home so I won't forget even one word. Honest."

Rudy looked at the faces around the table. Their
lips were set in straight lines. He could feel their eyes
piercing his skin, hear their thoughts buzz like angry

hornets. "I'll be a new person starting now," Rudy pleaded. "Give me half a chance."

"You've used up your chances," Mr. Alvarez said. "If I *ever* see you in this office or hear from Ms. Throckmeir that your behavior or your schoolwork is not your best—"

"*I* expect your complete attention in class," interrupted Ms. Throckmeir, "and participation in every activity, including Saturday's Carnival for Computers."

"No Nintendo. No TV," said Rudy's mom. "Schoolwork, chores, and church. Period!"

"Remember, Son, we're not looking for a change on the outside only," said Rudy's dad. "We also expect a change of attitude on the *inside*."

"The superintendent, Dr. Yasuzawa, is particularly interested in Rudy's case," said Mr. Alvarez. "He's requested a top-level conference, during the carnival Saturday, to further assess the situation."

Clamping his teeth together so they wouldn't chatter, Rudy grunted and nodded at the appropriate places.

How long, he wondered, *will it take to become perfect*?

Chapter
2

Monday morning, Rudy had an appointment to have a small filling done before school. As soon as he spotted Dr. Mac, they both crouched, stuck up their right thumbs, and yelled, "It *might* be . . . it *could* be . . . it *is* . . . *a home run!*"

Rudy glanced up at the small card stuck on the corner of the supply cabinet. He'd memorized it weeks ago at youth group as all the kids figured out how they'd put the Scripture into action: "Man looks at the outward appearance, but the Lord looks at the heart" (1 Samuel 16:7).

He grinned. Dr. Mac's youth group shared a secret. Instead of hiking and fishing during their Thanksgiving camping trip, they planned to pitch their tents behind an old, peeling house in Lost Hill and repaint it for its elderly owners.

Only youth group members and their parents knew that what appeared to be an ordinary camping trip would really be a work project for needy people.

"Come on, Rudy! Give me a *challenge* this time!"

Usually, Dr. Mac got his baseball cards down from the shelf and let Rudy pick half a dozen, which he stood against bottles on the dental tray. When Rudy pointed to a card, Dr. Mac recited exactly what was on the card while he worked on his tooth.

Rudy chose the more obscure players, but Dr. Mac never missed a fact. To top it off, he could even relate a funny story about the player or describe his hobbies and family.

Afterward, Rudy got to choose a few cards from a special box. Not the valuable cards like Babe Ruth, of course, but something new to add to his collection.

Dr. Mac's office was under the glide path of an airport runway that was seldom used. They must have been repairing the regular runways this morning, because Rudy had to shake his head and wave toward the ceiling whenever a plane drowned out Dr. Mac's voice.

"After making two home runs, he . . . " (*Roar*)

"And the most exciting thing is . . . " (*Roar*)

Rudy rolled his eyes and pointed upward. Dr. Mac tapped on Rudy's month-old braces and looked serious. "Now listen up," he said.

"You have these metal braces . . . " (*Roar*)

"There might be a problem because of your new filling. You see . . . " (*Roar*)

" . . . so don't be surprised if it happens. Call me."

While Rudy picked his baseball cards, he wondered how anyone as nice as Dr. Mac had gotten stuck with a kid as flaky as Dr. Mac's daughter, who was in Rudy's classes at school and at church.

Gwenny MacDonald liked to play weird characters, and she changed roles as quick as you could say, "Baltimore Orioles." Sometimes, she was Vanna White on "Wheel of Fortune," sometimes, she turned into a tough cop on an undercover assignment. She switched personalities so often, Rudy never knew what to expect. One thing was sure, though. *Every one* of her personalities adored Rudy.

As he left Dr. Mac's office, he glanced at the clock. It was 9:20 and Ms. Throckmeir would be waiting for him. Today, he had to do everything right. No funny stuff. No fooling around as he had in the past. That was over. Being perfect was going to take total concentration. Maybe Charlie would lay off now that he knew what the stakes were. Rudy had sworn him to secrecy over the weekend.

He jogged the ten blocks to school in record time. It was funny how things turned out, but Rudy had listened to the Series every opening day for the past three years.

In third grade, he'd scratched his chicken pox while lying on the sofa and watching the game on television.

In fourth grade, he sprained his ankle when he'd hurtled off his skateboard after breakfast. His mom bought a big carton of fudge chunk ice cream on the way back from the doctor and let him stay home from school.

Last year, he had developed a violent headache that included stabbing pains and dizziness. Fortunately, Mom had a party to cater, so Gram picked him up. He lay on her bed in a darkened room, his radio under the pillow. His headache lasted exactly as long as the ball game.

But today—well, his body had better be in his seat at school. Where his mind would be—that was the problem.

Rudy had to know what was going on. *Who was at bat? When should he hold his breath and pray?* He felt sick that the Orioles had to play, today, without his being with them . . . *straining* . . . *hoping* . . . *sweating* through each moment.

He opened the classroom door a slit and slid through silently, placing his admit slip from the office on Ms. Throckmeir's desk.

The seating arrangement was in the form of a square: two desks deep on sides one through three, with Ms. Throckmeir's desk forming the fourth side. She usually roamed about the center space, observing the students and giving help as needed. This morning, she was bent over Colleen's desk, her back to the door.

Everyone else noticed Rudy, though. Kim Yang and Shandra Washington smiled; Morton gave him a high five as he passed, and Gwenny batted her short, blond eyelashes at him. Her hair stood on end—sort of like a dandelion gone to seed. She kissed her fingers and blew the kisses toward Rudy. Charlie raised his eyebrows until his eyeballs protruded, so Rudy ran his hands down his body, flattening his pockets and shaking his head to indicate he wouldn't be giving the play-by-play.

"That's all we have time for today," Ms. Throckmeir told the class. "Take out your math books and fresh paper."

The assignment sprawled across the chalkboard in spiky cursive:

Test. Pages 149-151.

Rudy pawed through his desk until he found his math book under a mountain of paper. The book was open, some pages folded in on themselves, a couple of them loose. He flicked the loose pages back into the desk and scribbled his name at the top of his paper. Furtively, he scanned the room.

All he saw were heads bent over math papers. Nobody dared to look around during Ms. Throckmeir's tests. Once, Charlie had a nosebleed—sort of a geyser with blood spraying in the air—and Ms. Throckmeir stuffed a wad of tissues in his hand and told him he could go to the clinic *after* he finished the test.

The Novocain was wearing off. Rudy's left cheek

and chin prickled. He could twist his mouth some now. He swung his lips as far left as possible. Then, just as his upper and lower teeth met, he heard it:

"Hey, wise guy—ya wanna smack in the face?" Rudy almost jumped out of his seat. He peered at his classmates. Nobody looked up. He could hear only the sound of pencils scratching on the tests.

Rudy tried problem number one: "If a westbound train leaves New York City at 9:00 . . ."

He twisted his mouth to the left again and let his teeth touch. *"You double-cross me and you'll end up in the river, wearin' cement overshoes."* Rudy's heart was beating like a tom-tom. He chanced a glance out of the corner of his eye. Ms. Throckmeir was looking right at him. His head felt transparent—like one of those telephones with the jumble of colored wires sold in the mall.

Could she read his mind? Could she hear what was going on in his head? He bent over the book: "If a westbound train . . . " Maybe he could draw little squares to represent the trains.

Rudy heard Ms. Throckmeir's heels rap off toward the windows. Cautiously, he moved his lips to the side, prudently keeping his focus on his paper. This time, he twisted his teeth so far to the left that his eyes crossed. A click in his jaw marked the moment his uppers and lowers connected, like the distinct sound of a lock opening to the right key.

"Watch it, Buster. This thing's loaded." Rudy lifted

his prickly lips away from his teeth like a horse, and the mobster's maniacal laughter swelled.

Heads turned. Rudy cupped a hand over his mouth as if to cover a yawn and dropped his lips. Faces turned back to the tests. Purposeful hammer taps from Ms. Throckmeir's heels grew louder. Rudy's breath came in shallow, gasping spurts as he hunched over his math book.

Ms. Throckmeir's shadow formed a shroud over Rudy. Instinctively, he curled his arm around his paper. She stood watching him for what seemed like a lifetime. Then Ms. Throckmeir bent until her face was only a foot away from Rudy's.

Should he look back? He couldn't. A tickle started deep in his throat. He tried to swallow, but his spit had turned to cotton. The cough burst from his mouth before he got his hand over his lips. Rudy stared in horror as the droplets landed on Ms. Throckmeir's upper lip and lashes.

She flushed tomato red, and her breath poured around his face.

"You've done only one problem," she growled. "After school today. Until you complete the test."

The timer on Ms. Throckmeir's desk signaled gym. Rudy tested his teeth again and his heart soared. A magic mouth! Power! Sheer, raw power at his command!

He leaped to his feet and slid neatly into line behind good old Charlie.

Chapter

3

Following in line, Rudy felt a thumb run down his spine. Gwenny. He braced himself. She trotted beside him, matching one of his strides with two of her own. Today, she wore lensless glasses with chartreuse frames. A purple sparkle pencil stuck out behind her ear.

"How come you came in late this morning?"

"I had someplace to go," Rudy said vaguely.

"I figured that. Where did you go?"

Gwenny the Curious. Gwenny the Nosy. Gwenny the Snoop.

"Downtown."

"What for?"

Rudy started to hum. Loud enough to irritate her.

Gwenny snorted. "You just don't want me to know that my dad filled your tooth this morning. You were his first appointment."

He pictured himself giving her a hard shove.

She grabbed the purple pencil and flipped open a

notebook. "Since I'm carnival chairperson for our class, I'm signing everyone up for the early morning-shift. Do you want to nail booths, make posters, paint backdrops, or . . . ?"

"None of the above."

Rudy hated Gwenny's organizer role. She actually puffed herself up and swaggered. Naturally, she set her own rules for everybody to follow.

"You don't have much choice. Remember what Mr. Alvarez said at the assembly on Friday. It's our only chance to raise money for a computer lab."

Rudy hummed louder.

"There isn't time to fool around. The carnival starts at ten o'clock Saturday morning. All the sixth grade teachers supervised in the gym this morning. Everybody came except you."

They rounded the corner to the gym.

"Ms. Throckmeir said she was *positive* you'd help."

Rudy's neck prickled. Participation. It might show Ms. Throckmeir his progress toward perfection.

"Sure." He gulped. "I could even come in at six o'clock."

In gym, Rudy and Charlie lucked out. Usually, test day was boring. Mr. Spinelli sat at the end of the gym and marked his checklist as one student at a time ran the obstacle course, climbed the ropes, and performed on the balance beam.

Everybody had to sit in line and shut up so Mr.

Spinelli could concentrate. But today, his student teacher, Ms. O'Keefe, bent over the clipboard also. She frowned and shook her head. Neither one noticed Rudy and Charlie sitting together—something usually forbidden.

Rudy pressed his twisted mouth against Charlie's ear and opened his lips.

"*Stephen*," said a silken voice, "*I knew you'd come back to me some day. S-s-smooch.*"

"*Wow!*" Charlie whispered. "How'd you do that?"

Rudy shrugged. "I don't know. I moved my mouth around in math and when my new filling hit a certain place, it just happened."

"How come Ms. Throck didn't hear?"

Rudy grinned. "I've got *control*, man. If I keep my lips closed, I'm the only one who can hear it. If I open my lips, other people can hear too."

Shandra turned around and made cow eyes at Charlie. "Be sure to watch me," she whispered. "It'll bring me luck." She started around the obstacle course.

Charlie and Rudy slid back to the end of the line.

"Hey," Charlie said. "You can pass us the play-by-play like we planned."

"No way! I can't chance it, Charlie. You *know* what could happen."

Charlie's eyes sparked like black agates. "You owe us, Rudy. We didn't bust our guts inventing baseball sign language all summer for nothin'. You sign the game to me and Morton across the room like we did Friday. We'll write the key words on slips and pass them on."

"But . . ."

"'Course, Morton'll have to use Gwenny again, but she'd rather die than rat. You *are* her 'Rough 'n Ready Rudy,' you know."

Rudy stuck out his tongue and gagged. A hand shot back and grabbed his knee. Gwenny's soft giggle spurted out.

"Rudy's sick. Rudy's sick. Call for Gwenny, quick, quick, quick."

"Cut it out, Gwenny," Rudy said. "Charlie and I have important business to discuss."

"*Ooooh?* And what might that be?" Gwenny stepped into her Miss Manners role, raising her eyebrows and looking down her nose at Rudy. "Did I hear you say something about needing my help?"

"Look," Charlie said. "We're gonna handle the game today the same as Friday. You pass the plays from Morton to Kevin the regular way."

"Where's your radio?" Gwenny asked Rudy.

"Well, when your dad filled my tooth this morning . . . um . . ."

"What he's trying to tell you," said Charlie, "isn't important. It doesn't have anything to do with his teeth. Rudy has this amazing power, see? He concentrates hard enough and gets a 3-D picture in his mind. It's like he's there. Isn't that so, Rudy?"

"Um . . . yeah. Sure! I discovered a way to be in two places at once. This afternoon I'm going to the game, but I'll be in class at the same time."

Gwenny narrowed her green eyes. "You're lying, Rudy. And I won't pass your dumb messages if you don't tell me what's going on."

"It only happens when I do this." Rudy twisted his jaw to the left, clamped his lips shut and rocked back and forth like a mesmerized cobra. He knew Gwenny couldn't stand not knowing how things worked.

Suddenly, his eyes widened with disbelief. "Left fielder Bud Thompson's in the hospital," he told Charlie. "A bus crunched his car this morning on the way to the stadium."

"You made that up," said Gwenny. "Either that or you've got earphones."

But the boys had already tuned her out.

During lunch recess, Rudy argued with the boys who clotted around him.

"No way, you guys. I've got no more chances with Ms. Throck. Zip."

"All she can do is hang you up by your thumbs," joked Rusty.

"Scared?" asked Kevin.

"What about keeping your promises?" grumbled Morton.

"Seventh Street Sluggers stick together," said Eddie, scowling.

"A real buddy wouldn't let his friends down," Tony said.

Rudy put his hands over his ears and closed his eyes. "Stop!" he yelled. "You don't understand."

When the whistle blew, Gwenny skidded into line behind Rudy. Quick as a snake, she popped her index fingers into Rudy's ears. She gasped.

"You don't have any . . . there's nothing in your ears."

Rudy leaned close to her and lifted his lips.

" . . . *first game will be played in honor of Bud Thompson, who underwent surgery this morning.*"

Gwenny's freckles seemed to stand out from her nose in awe. For once, she didn't have anything to say.

The afternoon went according to plan. During social studies, Ms. Throckmeir sat at her desk on the fourth side of the square and graded papers. From his desk, back row on side three, Rudy listened to his teeth and signed to Morton and Charlie at their front row desks on sides one and two. They jotted down the plays and slipped the notes to the next students.

Gwenny passed notes like a born spy. Of course, Ms. Throckmeir never suspected Gwenny MacDonald, Star Student.

Most of the kids shot out of the door when the final bell rang, racing home to catch the rest of the game, but Gwenny bent over Rudy and waited, while he dug around in his desk for the unfinished math test.

"Oh, Rudy! It's so thrilling what you do with your mouth. Let me hear it one more time."

Rudy put his mouth up to Gwenny's ear and burped.

"I hate you, Rudy Benson," she screamed and tore off down the hall.

Charlie and Morton folded over and howled.

Chapter
4

"Rudy? There's a girl on the phone," yelled Mom.

Rudy shot out of bed like a rock from a slingshot.

"Mom," he shouted. "I forgot to tell you. Old Throck—I mean Ms. Throckmeir—wants us at school by seven every morning this week to work on the carnival."

"Hi." Gwenny's voice was as soft and silky as a cat's back. "Guess who won the purse yesterday?"

Rudy felt his chest tighten. "You?"

"Umhumm. I'm going to spend it in such a special way. You may take me to Denny's Dairy Delight every afternoon this week."

"Me? Take you? I don't think . . ."

"You don't need to think about this," she purred. "It's simply what is going to happen. I want a double chocolate sundae with chocolate peanut-butter ice cream and chocolate sprinkles. Right after school. Of course, you can have something too, but people will have to think *you* are taking *me*."

"No way!"

"My hands get *terribly tired* when I pass the notes, Rudy. Without some encouragement, I might be too weak to hide them so well. . . . "

Rudy slammed down the phone, snatched his clothes from the closet and plunged downstairs. He glanced at the clock and groaned. It was 6:50, and at a dead run, he could get to school in about sixteen minutes. Add on time to dress . . .

He scrambled into his clothes. Mom's voice floated down the hall.

"I have a dinner to cater tonight, Rudy, so you're on your own. Be sure to take a key."

It took extra seconds to snatch the front door key from the hook in the kitchen, but he made up for it by running a shortcut to school through Mrs. Weatherby's back lot.

He burst through the gym door and skidded to a stop. Charlie and Morton were pounding nails into the backdrop for the bottle throw. Kids from all fifth and sixth-grade classes were painting, stapling, and joking around. Rudy tried to spot Ms. Throckmeir.

"Charlie, did Ms. Throck notice I was . . . ?"

"Nah." Charlie grinned. "Someone from Mr. Anderson's class knocked over a paint can and she's been helping Mr. A clean it up."

Grabbing a paintbrush, Rudy slapped blue paint on one of the booths, stroking in time to the rumbling in his stomach.

* * * * *

The first note came at 9:30. Rudy knew by its ragged pink edges that the bit of paper had been read by everyone between Gwenny's desk and his:

"*Rudy. You were soooo nice on the phone this morning.*"

The second arrived a few minutes later: "*Rudy. I'm thrilled you invited me to have ice cream with you after school today. Shall we keep it our personal secret?*"

There were definite snickers now. By noon, Rudy had fielded six love notes and a candy heart stamped, "*You're It, Baby.*"

At five minutes after twelve, Tony Perez slid another paper scrap across Rudy's desk. Ms. Throckmeir unexpectedly turned her head.

"Rudy, show me that note."

"What note, Ms. Throckmeir? I haven't been passing notes." *Just getting them*, he thought. She turned to put the eraser back on the chalkboard rail and started toward him.

Rudy held up his hands. "Nothing here, honest, Ms. Throckmeir." He flipped out his pockets and put thirty-seven cents, two rubber bands, and a pack of baseball cards on his seat.

Screech! Ms. Throckmeir yanked up the lid to his desk and rummaged around to reveal only school supplies and four overdue library books.

Rudy gulped. The pink paper ball, like the others, hurt as it sank slowly from his throat to his stomach.

"I thought you were a goner," Morton said at lunch.

"Hey, place your bets," interrupted Charlie. "If you don't ante up, we won't have a big enough purse." Charlie hauled the envelope out of his back pocket.

"Not today," said Kevin. "I'm flat broke."

Tony scowled. "I'm not kicking in. Not when a girl won our $8.50 yesterday."

Charlie shook the envelope under Rudy's nose. "Put your money where your magic mouth is," he ordered.

"You have a short memory," Rudy shouted. "Bottom line—my money goes for the camping trip, and I stay out of trouble."

He turned his head so no one would see the sudden tears that sprang to his eyes. Obviously, money was Charlie's best friend, not Rudy.

Suddenly, he felt butterflies in his stomach—and not about the purse. There was something wrong . . . something important . . .

"It should be clear sailing by the time the game comes on," Charlie was telling the guys. "I figure Ms. Throck will get our science reports out of the way right after lunch."

"Oh no!" Rudy yelled. "I forgot my hamster report. Gotta go."

He glanced hungrily at his tray—soup, salad, and lemon pudding—nothing he could take with him. He raced home, grabbed his report, and dashed back to school in time to see the last of the sixth graders disappear into the school.

"Hey!" shouted Mr. Spinelli. He was outside teaching the first graders to play dodgeball. "You need an admit slip from Mr. Alvarez."

Rudy's stomach knotted like a fist. No matter how hard he tried, he struck out. The adults expected perfection; Charlie drove him crazy with his gambling schemes; the guys wouldn't let him off the hook about the play-by-play. And Gwenny—after-school ice cream *dates*? He cringed at the thought.

"You left the school grounds without permission," said Mr. Alvarez, his hand reaching for the phone. "Is there any reason why I shouldn't call your parents?"

Rudy hauled out the damp report from under his T-shirt. "I forgot my hamster report, sir, but that was because I wrote it Saturday and did the pictures and the typing Sunday."

Mr. Alvarez read through the report page by page, scrutinizing the detailed charts and drawings. "You know a lot about hamsters," he said. "I used to breed them myself. Tell me, have you ever crossed a Teddy Bear hamster with a Golden?"

"Not yet, Mr. Alvarez, but I'd like to."

Mr. Alvarez leaned back in his chair. "This is an outstanding report, Rudy. You can be proud of yourself. If you want to discuss future breeding projects, stop in and see me."

Rudy strode down the hall to class. Man to man. It felt great. Maybe he'd drop by the office with his newest litter in a couple of weeks.

He checked in on the game and discovered the Orioles already had a man on first and McNally was at bat. *Crack!* A base hit took him to first and Blair to second. Rudy held his breath and sent up a prayer. But did he dare listen to the game? A roar from his teeth interrupted. The teams were tied now, with the opposing team coming up to bat.

Rudy ignored his friends during Shandra Washington's ostrich report.

By the end of the third inning, the Orioles were in deep trouble.

"It's Brooks Robinson up for the Orioles, two men on base, two outs.

If Robinson can break the tie . . . "

"Rudy? Time for your report," said Ms. Throckmeir. *What rotten timing! In a few more seconds . . .*

"My report is on hamsters." Rudy stood in front of the class and read aloud, holding his folder in front of his face.

"Fly missed by the catcher," he said. "Error."

"What?" asked Ms. Throckmeir.

"Um—I meant some hamsters catch flies. Sort of like dessert, you know."

" . . . anyway, both hamsters preferred sugar water to regular water. Home run!"

"Rudy, show me that report," said Ms.

Throckmeir. "It doesn't make sense."

"Sorry, Ms. Throckmeir, I read the wrong words. It should be *at home*, I made some *runs* for the hamsters—for exercise, you know."

Rudy couldn't say how he made it through the report, but when he returned to his seat, he looked intently at Ms. Throckmeir and ignored Charlie and Morton's frantic signals.

Suddenly, he realized that his oral and written reports wouldn't match. What if Ms. Throckmeir went on memory when she graded him and never examined his graphs and breeding lists?

"Please, Ms. Throckmeir. I've got to read my report again."

As Rudy started reading, Dr. Yasuzawa walked in and perched on a chair in the back of the room.

Minutes later, out of the limelight, Rudy twisted his mouth to keep up with the action. He bent over his creative writing paper, afraid to meet the Seventh Street Sluggers' eyes. Giving the play-by-play wasn't worth the risk. He worked steadily until the final bell rang.

Over the noise of desks slamming and students leaving, he heard:

" . . . facial contortions . . . strange, spastic mouth movements . . . school psychologist . . . " His heart sank.

It sounded like Dr. Yasuzawa was back on his case.

Chapter

5

Rudy nibbled his nails as he waited outside the girl's bathroom. His pockets bulged with $8.50 in coins from Gwenny's winnings. Add on his house key and his pants hung perilously low under the weight. Whenever he moved, he sounded like a tin can full of marbles.

Charlie whacked him on the back. "We're here to protect you, buddy." He looked like a wise old bird in his round glasses.

"I can't believe you're taking her on a date," Morton stated for the fifth time.

"Dum-dum-de-dum . . . " intoned Eddie, closing his eyes and crossing his arms across his chest like a corpse.

Rusty swished his hips. Tony and Kevin laughed.

The door burst open and Gwenny's friends spilled out. Rudy could hear his heart thudding in the sudden silence as Gwenny appeared.

She wore a pink, shiny dress loaded with lace.

Her pale hair stood up stiff with gel and topped with flowers. Silver question marks dangled from her earlobes. "Y'all ready?" she asked in a Southern drawl. "Colleen, if you can carry ma li'l old backpack . . ."

Gwenny hung on Rudy's arm and fluttered her eyelashes.

"What an unexpected surprise. I'll bet you even found out what my favorite dessert is, you sneaky thing."

"Yahooo," howled Morton, dancing backward in front of them.

"Shut up, dunce," snapped Shandra. She walked close to Charlie and matched her steps with his, creating a single shadow.

"Gwenny says you want to take her out every day," called Kim.

"Right to the loony bin," yelled Tony.

They massed through the door of Denny's Dairy Delight jostling and joking.

Rudy and Gwenny sat in the center booth. The guys crowded into the one behind Rudy, and Gwenny's friends knelt on the seat of the third booth and hung over Gwenny's shoulder.

Mr. Denny, whose white-aproned stomach rounded like a giant scoop of his own vanilla ice cream, ambled over with an order pad.

"Well? What'll it be?"

Rudy opened his mouth and gasped, "We want to eat."

"I figured that," Denny said.

The girls giggled.

Rudy took a deep, shuddering breath. "Ice cream. Chocolate. No. Chocolate-peanut butter. With stuff on the top."

"Chocolate sauce," Gwenny mouthed silently.

"Chocolate sauce." Rudy's mind froze. Gwenny kicked him under the table.

"Oh, yeah. Whipped cream."

"Chocolate sprinkles," Gwenny prompted soundlessly.

"Chocolate sprinkles . . ."

Rudy's eyes followed Gwenny's lips as he spoke. "Two cherries so we can share . . ."

The guys hooted. Rudy felt his face go hot. "And a strawberry shake for me."

The sundae rose like a giant mountain, running with chocolate rivers and standing in a fudge lake. A glacier of whipped cream cradled two shiny cherries.

Gwenny's spoon sculpted the mound, snagging a cherry and carrying it through the whipped cream, the chocolate-peanut butter ice cream and into the fudge puddle.

Jennifer leaned over her shoulder and opened her mouth. *Whack!* Her head hit Gwenny's.

Splat! The ice cream landed with a plop on Gwenny's chin, then skied slowly down the front of her dress, leaving a chocolate trail. When the ice cream reached Gwenny's lap, her eyes bugged.

Rudy lost it. His laugh burst out in a spray of strawberry shake.

Gwenny grabbed her backpack from Colleen and charged for the ladies' room.

"Everybody out," bellowed Denny, and the kids shot out of the shop leaving Rudy sucking hungrily on his straw and trying to figure out what to do.

Finally, he ordered chocolate cake à la mode and another shake.

Sometime between the end of the cake and the middle of the shake, Gwenny emerged. She wore paint-spattered jeans and the sweatshirt she'd torn while working on the carnival backdrop.

"Sorry about what happened," said Rudy. "If Jennifer hadn't . . . "

"I know." Gwenny spooned up melted ice cream and sighed. "We should have come alone. Or maybe, not at all. When Charlie asked to borrow a dollar, I didn't even know it was for the football pool." A tear wiggled down her cheek and she brushed it away.

"Nah, it's okay. I was starving anyway . . . "

A second tear trickled down Gwenny's other cheek.

"Hey, it's not a disaster," Rudy said uncomfortably. "I skipped breakfast to work on the carnival and missed lunch because I left my hamster report at home. Really—you're doing me a favor."

"Maybe, even saving your life, huh?" Gwenny's familiar smile popped back into place.

"I thought you gave a great science report today. You know, I took care of Colleen's hamster last summer, but it escaped in my room, which was sort of a mess. Anyway, I didn't catch him until Colleen got back from camp."

"There's a trick to it," said Rudy, slurping the last of his second shake. "Put down the cardboard tube from a paper towel roll. A hamster will crawl inside to hide and then you've got him."

"You're good at a lot of things, Rudy. Especially baseball. I got so excited when you made the winning run the day before school started, I almost fell over."

"You saw the game? I don't remember seeing you last summer except at church."

"I watched all of your games, Rudy. And you weren't supposed to see me. I wore disguises."

"You want a refill, kid?" shouted Denny. Rudy gave him a thumbs up.

Gwenny giggled. "Once, I wore a gray wig and my grandma's spectacles. But I had to keep an old blanket around me so my shorts wouldn't show. I almost got heatstroke."

"Why do you keep changing clothes?" asked Rudy. "And personalities? I'm not even sure who you really are."

"Well, remember our Scripture in youth group," Gwenny said defensively. "'Man looks on the outward appearance, but the Lord looks at the heart.' So it only matters what God sees. Right?"

"That's not true. Most of your personalities are really dumb. But I like you, well—ordinary. The way you are now."

Gwenny blinked and scraped the last of the sundae from the bottom of her bowl. She scratched around so long, Rudy wondered which would wear out first—the spoon or the glass.

"Rudy—you know about Clyde, my sister Margaret's fiancé, don't you?"

"Yeah. Your dad told me he's in the minors. It must be great to know a real pro—I mean to talk to whenever you want, and all."

"He's coming to dinner Friday night. Would you like to meet him?"

A score of questions bubbled up in Rudy's mind. Things he wanted to know about pro ball. Tips he needed to play better. The inside story on . . .

"You could come at six."

"You bet! On the dot. Or how about five-thirty? Or five?"

But Gwenny had already picked up her backpack and started for the door. "It's a sure thing," she called over her shoulder. "And don't forget our ice cream date tomorrow."

Rudy stood in a golden glow while Denny rang up the bill. Blindly, he emptied his pockets onto the counter and scooped up the change without looking.

Friday *might* be . . . *could* be . . . the most important day of his life!

Chapter 6

Rudy leaped out of bed when the alarm rang the next morning. Even the rain couldn't dampen his spirits.

I'm going to meet Clyde Reilly! Rudy's thoughts soared as he wolfed down his breakfast. Wait till he told the guys. They'd be panting with envy. He pictured it in detail. The guys would be out on the playground swapping stories. Eddie would spot Rudy's faraway look.

"Hey, Rudy."

He wouldn't answer.

Charlie would snap his fingers in front of Rudy's eyes.

"He doesn't even blink."

"Is he listening to his teeth?"

"Uh-uh. See how his mouth's hanging open?"

"Looks like he's in a trance."

"Maybe he's pretending."

"Let's tickle him." That would be Rusty.

He'd come to, then. Maybe look around like he

was dazed. "Just thinking."

"About what?"

"My friend, Clyde Reilly. What we'll talk about when I see him Friday night."

Gasp!

"Clyde Reilly's your friend?"

"Yeah. We're having dinner together."

"Can we come?"

"No," he'd say vaguely. "Clyde needs his privacy. It'll just be family and a few close friends."

Maybe later, he'd introduce his teammates. One at a time. Give 'em a thrill.

Had he forgotten anything? His backpack held his math book and yesterday's homework. Suddenly, Rudy felt his stomach twang like a broken guitar string. The money for Gwenny's ice cream!

He raced upstairs.

There on his dresser, sat the uncounted change from the money he'd given Mr. Denny yesterday. A quarter, a nickel, and four pennies. He'd eaten up the whole $8.50! And he had to take Gwenny to Denny's Dairy Delight three more days!

Panic set in. He started jerking out his dresser drawers and dumping the contents on his bed. He fished through the mess and came up with a dime and three pennies.

Wildly, he looked around his room. His baseball cards! He emptied the box on the carpet by his closet and crawled around spreading them out. None of the ordinary cards—but what about Sandy Kofax? Morton had offered him $2 for it last week. And Tony kept asking to see Bob Gibson. What could he get for that one? He picked three more, just in case, and ran down the stairs. These were his prize cards, but he could do extra chores and replace them later. Right now, he would keep his part of the bargain with Gwenny—and Friday night—he'd meet Clyde.

He dashed down the block, his backpack jerking against the straps. What if Mrs. MacDonald said no? What if Gwenny changed her mind? What if . . . ?

He charged through the gym door at full speed and smacked into Gwenny. They both rebounded onto the hardwood floor.

"Eeeeow," she screamed. "You really pack a wallop."

Gwenny rubbed the rear of her black tights and jammed a French beret back on her head. "It's okay about Friday—and you can come at five. Your parents, too. My mom's calling your mom this morning."

Rudy scrambled to his feet, still panting. "*All right!*"

The guys ambled up. Kevin smirked and stuck his nose in the air.

"Parley voo Fransay?" Charlie asked. He wiggled his eyebrows.

"Oo-la-la," crooned Morton. "Weel you paint my peek-ture, Madam Moyzel?"

Gwenny ignored them and whispered in Rudy's ear. "Let's ditch everybody and go alone today."

Rudy gulped. There had to be a way. Miracles still happened—didn't they?

"Okay, " he promised. Her smile, warm as sunshine, rewarded him as she disappeared into the crowd.

Tony held up an imaginary palette with one hand and scrubbed an invisible brush around in a little circle. "Sill Voo Play, Rudee. Stand steel, and I weel mak you a buety-fool portrait."

"Cut it out," snapped Rudy. "She's okay once you get to know her."

Rusty pulled a face and nodded. "Sure thing. She's one hundred percent nuts. One hundred percent of the time."

Rudy blew out his breath in exasperation.

A whistle shrilled, and Ms. Throckmeir beckoned to Rudy. He trotted down to the far end of the gym. She handed him a hammer and put him to work reinforcing the puppet theater.

Today, travel day for the teams, meant no hassle from the guys about broadcasting a game. He patted his pocket. The baseball cards nestled there like a slim wad of bills. Gwenny seemed like a new friend. And soon, he would meet Clyde.

Ms. Throckmeir wandered from one booth to another. The left bow of her glasses had broken, and she held up the lens on that side with her fingers.

Rudy could tell from the way she kept tilting her head that she was trying to find which of her trifocal lenses to look through. When the bell rang, she stumbled over a piece of wood, and her glasses sailed across the gym and broke apart at the middle.

The class wrote all morning. Spelling. Math. Journals. Book reports.

Ms. Throckmeir sat and stared blindly into space.

At lunchtime, Rudy traded Charlie his chocolate ice cream for one of Mrs. Freeman's peanut butter cookies. Tony gave him half a pastrami sandwich for his cafeteria soup.

"How about an egg?" Rusty grinned, cradling the slimy white mound in his grubby hand. Everybody knew Rudy despised eggs.

"Hey, Tony. Remember my Bob Gibson? I'll sell him to you for a dollar. And that's at half off."

"Yeah! But I gave Charlie my money for tomorrow's game. Maybe after the Series."

"Anyone? Morton? I'll make you a deal you can't resist on Sandy Kofax."

"You bet!" Morton's eyes clouded. "Make that later," he said. "I've got all my money in the pool."

"Buy the card now, and earn your game money after school."

"Well . . . "

"The price doubles after today."

Charlie slapped his hand against his pocket and glared at Rudy. "The money stays right here where it's supposed to be. That bet's a done deal."

"I need money today. Like *now*!"

"So you can take Gwenny out?"

"What of it?" Rudy challenged. His fist hammered the table. Too bad it wasn't Charlie's face.

Charlie shrugged and licked his spoon.

*   *   *   *   *

Rudy wasn't surprised when a substitute teacher met them after lunch.

"My name is Mr. Willowby," the man wheezed, pulling out a handkerchief and blowing his nose. "Ms. Throckmeir left instructions for you to work in groups to finish the carnival posters."

Charlie and Morton shoved toward Rudy, but Gwenny got there first.

She looked at Rudy with a tentative smile. "Partners?"

Somewhere, along with her beret, she'd lost her French accent. It took him a moment to realize that this was the real Gwenny.

"Sure," he said.

They lay on their stomachs, head to head across the poster, filling in the penciled lines with fluorescent paints. Rudy carefully stacked his five prize baseball cards beside him so they wouldn't wrinkle in his pocket.

"What's on those cards?"

"The lowdown on each player. How well he bats, how many runs he's made. That sort of thing."

Gwenny reached for the cards, examined them, and laid them out in a straight line.

"I like Al Kaline best. And it's a tie between Tom Seaver and Sandy Kofax for second choice. The rest aren't anything special."

"But Bob Gibson was Most Valuable Player that year and Bud Thompson . . . "

"So? Al Kaline looks like you. And he has dreamy blue eyes. Bud Thompson has a mean little face. He looks like a wife beater."

Rudy sighed. Guys and girls sure looked at things differently.

"Eee-aah, eee-aah!"

Charlie's braying laughter brought the substitute teacher to his feet. Rudy peeked over the bookcase.

Morton's face twisted grotesquely like he'd run into a brick wall, but Rudy could tell that the flood of red dripping from his nostrils matched the tempera paint on his brush. Charlie sported a set of metallic gold freckles. The largest one trickled downward like a tear.

Rudy felt a flush of embarrassment as he watched Morton's stork legs pumping up and down in fake fury. Suddenly, he realized that if it hadn't been for Gwenny's offer, he'd be part of that work group. He shivered.

Gwenny reached for the blue paint. "Have you

saved up enough for the camping trip?"

"Not yet, but I'm close."

"Me, too. I baby-sit the Jenkins kids on Wednesday nights so their parents can go to leadership group at church."

"Those brats? Lonnie Jenkins gets sent to the office so often I feel like he works there. And it seems like every time I'm in the hall, Derek is sitting on the bench by the kindergarten."

Gwenny giggled. "Kayla is worse than the two of them put together. She's three, and she'll be an Olympic runner when she grows up. That is, *if* I let her live that long! Last Wednesday she smeared herself with margarine and climbed into the oven. She told me she was a turkey getting ready for Thanksgiving."

They shifted the poster to get a better angle. "I can hardly wait to meet the new girl. She was supposed to be in youth group Sunday, but she never showed."

"Another girl?" Rudy teased. "We need more guys for the team."

Gwenny stuck her tongue out at him. "Her name is Darlene or Darla or something—my dad couldn't read the registration form, but her last name is Stratton. Her grandmother left six messages at the church, but no phone number. I wonder if she'll be in our class here, too."

Rudy shrugged. "We have more girls than Mr.

Anderson's class. She'll probably end up there."

Periodically, as they talked, Rudy checked in with his teeth. Mostly, he heard ads for denture cleaners or deodorant. Then the program returned to a soap opera. A romantic scene. It wasn't hard to figure out what was coming. Slyly, Rudy leaned across the poster and lifted his lips. A man's deep-pitched voice traveled across the room at high volume.

"Come on, baby. I'll show you how a real man kisses."

The entire class froze in silence.

Obediently, Gwenny closed her eyes and puckered up. She had a blissful look on her face.

The class erupted into a herd of trumpeting elephants.

Gwenny leaped up. "You're disgusting," she shouted at everyone.

"Back to work," roared Mr. Willowby. "What's your name, young man?" He snatched a pad from Ms. Throckmeir's desk and wrote double time.

Before Rudy could retreat, Gwenny flopped down again. "Ignore those dopes. I liked it. Anyway, we're going to Denny's alone."

Rudy's face stiffened. "I . . . I don't have enough money to take you out. Remember I said you saved my life, yesterday? Well, all I have left is thirty-four cents."

Gwenny's mouth dropped open. No sound. No movement. Two tears welled up, giving her a froggy look. Was she in shock? Rudy's mind raced through all the 911 television shows he'd watched. Couldn't people die from shock?

"I tried to sell my best baseball cards," he said, "but no dice. I'll make it up to you, I promise."

"Promise, smomish! I trusted you . . . you . . . *rat heart*! I'll sue you for breach of promise. I'll throw your stupid baseball notes on the floor. I'll . . . " She slapped down her brush, grabbed the girl's room marker off the chalk rail, and shot out the door.

A rumbling filled Rudy's ears. He couldn't focus on the poster. Gwenny hated him and he deserved it. He could drop dead for all the guys cared. In trouble at school again. Saturday's conference loomed like a bottomless pit. And all because of these stupid teeth!

Scuffing through the leaves on the way home— the back way home—Rudy remembered Dr. Mac telling the youth group things never get so bad that God doesn't provide an escape route. When he reached the house, he ducked into the garage and yanked down Dad's "Pay Projects" list from the wall. Maybe, if he could get his homework out of the way before dinner . . .

Chapter
7

Rain sheeted down, smacking Rudy in the face whenever he tipped his head back far enough to see under the yellow hood on his raincoat. His cheeks bulged with blueberry muffin hunks and he tried to chew faster. Beneath his shirt, he felt the edges of the orange folder containing his extra-credit book report.

After only four hours of sleep, he staggered like a zombie, but his jeans carried $2.25 from the chores he'd done after dinner last night. At bedtime, he'd stuffed a towel under his door, read an abridged version of *Treasure Island*, and written his report. He figured he'd put it right under Mr. Willowby's note on the corner of Ms. Throckmeir's desk. Maybe they'd balance each other out.

Halfway across the playground he sighted Gwenny. With little droplets hanging from her frizzy, light hair, she looked like a wet fox.

"Got the money," Rudy shouted through the downpour. Gwenny squinted up at him as they splashed through the puddles. "Show me," she demanded.

When they got to the gym, Rudy hauled some bills and loose change out of his jeans pocket and tried to shove it into Gwenny's hand.

"*You* invited me, remember? *I'm* not going to pay. Not in public."

"Okay. So forget it. Just remember, I kept my word."

"Well—keep the money hidden until we get to Denny's."

Charlie and Rusty sauntered over. "You okay?" Rusty asked. "You look like road kill."

"I didn't get much sleep."

"You're *not* too beat to do the play-by-play," Charlie challenged.

Gwenny cocked her head. "I guess I *could* pass the notes today. I mean, knowing ice cream is coming up . . ."

"Great! It's settled," cried Charlie.

Rusty pounded him on the back. "I knew you wouldn't let us down."

Rudy chewed over Gwenny's offer all morning. He had lucked out on Tuesday, what with Dr. Yasuzawa observing in the room, and yesterday's team travel day had bought him some time. But today? He couldn't think of an out.

Ms. Throckmeir kept silent about Rudy's folder. It perched in the upper right corner of her desk where he'd put it earlier, but the note from Mr. Willowby had vanished.

Was she saving it to read aloud? Could she be ignoring his extra-credit work? He tried to imagine what Mr. Willowby had written about yesterday.

Dear Ms. Throckmeir: Please don't blame Rudy for disrupting the class. Charlie and Morton acted like idiots, but Rudy worked so hard. He and Gwenny got a lot done. It wasn't his fault that Gwenny puckered up and the class fell apart. He's a real great kid!

Sure. And Ms. Throckmeir will praise me sky high and tell all the teachers what a terrific student I am! Yes, Siree! Step right up, folks and take a look at Rudy the Reformed! Rudy the Perfect! Rudy the Saintly! Twenty-five cents a ticket! Get a good look!

Ms. Throckmeir's exasperated voice cut in. "We're waiting for your answer, Rudy."

Smothered giggles rippled across the room.

I won't pass the plays today, he decided. *Even if I lose all my friends.*

"Would you repeat the question, Ms. Throckmeir?"

*   *   *   *   *

Charlie and Morton spent lunch recess in the office because of yesterday's paint incident. The rain had stopped and sun shone on the playground's wet gravel. Rudy leaned against the wire fence and locked in on the game. The Seventh Street Sluggers huddled around him, and he lifted his lips so they could all hear.

"Robinson misses the ball!"

"Come on, Brooks," Eddie grunted. "You can do it!"

"Strike two! Nolan is in top form today. But both teams are playing superbly."

"Wow!" breathed Rusty.

"Already, at the bottom of the first, we can tell this might be the game of the season."

If someone missed a ball, he missed it by an inch. The opposition scored a home run by hitting the ball into the bleachers, so close to Blair's outstretched glove that for a moment, the announcer thought he'd caught it.

Inside, Rudy listened to his teeth and kept his eyes on Ms. Throckmeir, ignoring the guys' frantic signals. When she stood in profile, talking about African wildlife, he noticed how her nose moved up and down as she articulated the words. When her lips went down, her nostrils elongated like a baboon's. He stared in fascination.

"What do you think about that, Rudy?" Ms. Throckmeir turned to him expectantly.

Caught between third base and home plate, Rudy blinked and swallowed.

Before he could answer, the door opened and a woman shaped like a soda straw with spectacles and a black topknot bent over Ms. Throckmeir and whispered in her ear. A minute later, Rudy was trotting behind the woman down the hall.

"My name is Dr. Pokeberry. I'm a psychologist for the school district," she announced once Rudy was seated at the small table in front of her desk. Her mouth curved invitingly, but her eyes gave a one-false-move-and-you've-had-it look.

"I'm going to ask you some questions and give you a few puzzles to put together. Then you can do a paper and pencil test for me."

Rudy answered the questions quickly and slapped the puzzle pieces together in no time flat. *Step aside, Einstein!* Then, Dr. Pokeberry placed a thick test booklet and an answer sheet in front of him, and he groaned inwardly.

His last check-in with the game as they entered the office showed the score two and two with three men on base. How could he keep his mind on the test?

But he'd seen the shows on TV and knew what he was up against. Dr. Pokeberry would pretend to be working on papers, but she'd really be observing him. Timing him. Trying to analyze what was going on inside his head. He mustn't show any "spastic contortions," but the temptation to listen to his teeth overpowered him.

Quickly, Rudy stuck a pencil in the left side of his mouth. It rolled a little as he wrote, and he could still get his teeth in position for broadcast. His future flashed before him: fifteen years old, a baritone voice, still in sixth grade.

He removed the pencil and put a black marker between his teeth. He felt like one of those old guys puffing on a fat cigar.

Rudy could see from the corner of his eye that Dr. Pokeberry kept glancing at him while she wrote. His fingers shook. He tried to read the questions faster. Time probably counted a lot. As he bent over the test, he felt two warm puddles of saliva forming on his thighs. He was drooling. He probably looked like a pit bull waiting for lunch.

Dr. Pokeberry turned the page in her notebook. Rudy's neck prickled. He removed the marker and stuffed a chalkboard eraser between his teeth. At least it would absorb his saliva while it kept him out of trouble.

The test took a thousand years. When he marked his last answer and handed the paper to Dr. Pokeberry, he noticed a frown crumpling her brows into hairy mounds.

She leaned way over the desk like a long-necked bird with sad eyes. "You can tell me, Rudy. When your parents punish you, do they ever withhold food?"

*   *   *   *   *

" . . . *hush falls over the crowd as McRae steps up to*

the plate. This is the game of the century, folks. He swings . . ." By the time Rudy arrived at the classroom, no power on earth could have pried his jaws apart.

Like an oasis in the desert, the row of yellow and orange raincoats hanging above a welter of muddy boots offered protection. His psychological testing was going to take a long time today.

Charlie spotted Rudy's feet sticking out while en route to the boy's room and crawled in next to him under the raincoats.

"What's the score?"

"Mmm."

"Who's ahead?"

"Mmm."

He looked into Rudy's staring eyes and poked him. "Lift your lips."

" *. . . crowd goes wild. It's a home run for the Orioles! Wait! Rose threw all the way from . . . Out!"*

Charlie made a dash for the boy's room. Two minutes later, Eddie held the bathroom marker as he crouched beside Rudy.

"Strike three! Brooks Robinson doused for the first time by . . ."

Morton didn't even try for the boy's room when he charged out clutching the bathroom marker.

Ms. Throckmeir burst into the hall, passed the girl's room door, and knocked on the next one. "Morton, are you in there?"

The boys stared at each other in horror. "Run," Rudy whispered hoarsely, when Ms. Throckmeir marched back to the classroom. Morton bolted into the boy's room, and Rudy slid skillfully behind the line of raincoats until he sat beside the door to the girl's room.

Ms. Throckmeir reappeared with a meter stick. Starting at the far end of the coat hooks, she jabbed sharply between them. Her stick punched viciously against the wall each time she thrust. She didn't look up when a loud sound of flushing signaled Morton's exit from the bathroom.

Adrenaline shot through Rudy's veins. She knew! Ms. Throckmeir bent over a jumble of boots in front of the coats, stabbing viciously. Rudy flattened himself against the wall and crept into the recess leading to the nearest bathroom. He eased himself inside, locked the middle stall door behind him, and sat down shakily.

The final bell rang. Footsteps. Laughter. Suddenly, the door burst open and in trooped a bunch of girls. Gwenny's distinctive voice rang out above all the others.

"Listen, everyone. Rudy's going to kiss me today—here's how it'll work. Wait! I'd better make sure we're really alone."

Steps pattered toward the far stall. Rudy felt a sense of déjà vu—as though he had experienced this situation before. Grimly, he lifted both feet off the floor and let his bottom sink into the toilet's icy water. Gwenny's feet moved quickly past the closed door.

"It's all clear," she whispered. "Here's the plan. When Rudy takes me to Denny's today, I'll . . . " Her words dropped to a murmur.

"Oooh," came Jennifer's shrill voice. "You wouldn't dare!"

"I might try that on Charlie." Shandra's laughter bounced out like popcorn.

The girls giggled uncontrollably.

After the door slammed behind them, Rudy looked at his sports watch and waited a full thirty minutes before he felt the odds were in his favor. He hobbled across the tile floor, shivering, cold water streaming down his legs.

Poking his head out of the doorway, he assessed the situation. The hall seemed deserted. Cautiously, he tiptoed toward the nearest exit, leaving a trail of water behind.

"Hey, kid! You're messing up my floor," the janitor's voice roared, but Rudy didn't look back. He eased out of the school. If he kept to the alleys, maybe no one would see him.

He thought back to this morning and remembered Gwenny's eager face. She trusted him. Did her friends laugh when he didn't show up? He felt like a jerk. She'd never understand. And he couldn't tell her he'd been listening in the girl's bathroom.

Suddenly, warning sirens shrieked in his head. No one stood up Gwenny and survived unscathed. The only question was *how* she'd retaliate and *when*. What could she do? Cancel Clyde? Make a fool of him at the carnival?

Then warm relief enfolded him. At least she didn't know about Saturday's life-threatening conference. And what she didn't know, she couldn't sabotage.

Chapter 8

The Seventh Street Sluggers squatted around Tony, chewing furiously on the huge orange and black gumdrops he'd brought to celebrate winning the pool yesterday.

Morton danced around, slashing the air with a stick in place of a sword. " . . . and she stabbed that meter stick into the wall like she was fighting a duel."

"I planned to go next," said Rusty, "but she pocketed the boy's room marker."

"How come you didn't get caught, Rudy?" Eddie asked.

"Simple know-how."

"Come on. Tell us," Rusty demanded.

"Let's just say I knew what to do—something unforgettably awful—and I did it," Rudy snapped. "Subject closed."

"What a game!" Tony laughed. "Hope today's score won't be so close." He popped two more gumdrops in his mouth and passed the bag.

Rudy stared into space. He let the conversation flow around him like wind around a flagpole.

"Let's place our bets," said Charlie.

"Shorry," Tony said with the middle of his lips. "I don't have any money to bet today. I shpent it all on getting my glove repaired." With a gumdrop in each cheek, he looked like a chipmunk with mumps.

"Kevin? Morton?" They shook their heads.

"I've got it!" shouted Rusty. "Let's put up some fun stuff."

"Like?"

"Like I'll put up a movie ticket for Saturday."

"What's the movie?" asked Kevin.

"Um . . . I think it's something about ballet. My sister's got the flu, so . . . "

"Yuck!" Morton snorted. "I'll put up one of my butterflies. My pick."

"An overnight in my backyard," yelled Tony.

"A commemorative stamp," Kevin offered.

Charlie eyed Eddie. "How about your snakes?" he asked.

Eddie choked and spit out his gumdrops. "You've got to be kidding. Maybe the *loan* of them for a while."

"How long?"

"First, tell us what you have to offer, and I'll let you know."

Charlie bit his lip. "You're always complaining

about all the chores you have to do on Saturdays. How about if I did a Saturday of chores for the winner?"

Eddie bounced to his feet. "How about a *month* of Saturday chores? For a month of snakes?"

"Done!"

"Rudy?" Charlie demanded.

"I've got bad news for you guys. I'm having a conference tomorrow. Big time stuff. I've got to act perfect in school, today, so . . . I'm not going to sign the game."

Stunned silence. Disbelieving faces.

"You've got to. Teammates stick together," snapped Morton.

"You're saying we learned baseball sign language for nothing?"

"It's not that simple," Rudy protested.

"You chicken?"

"No, but—"

"*Traitor*," yelled Rusty.

"We had the perfect setup—until you started acting like a goody-goody girl!" roared Charlie. "You've turned into a real rotter."

Rudy took a deep breath. Charlie hit a sore point. *He'd* organized the Seventh Street Sluggers. *He'd* invented baseball sign language and figured out how to broadcast the game. They depended on him. Could he make them understand?

"Wait a minute, you guys," he croaked. "There's something you don't know."

One by one, he scanned their faces. One by one, they clamped their jaws shut and turned their faces away.

The day crawled by. No one spoke to Rudy except his teachers. His guts twisted. The guys were right. He'd let them down. He had changed for a reason they'd never understand.

He glanced at Gwenny. Her face held a thoughtful look. Gwenny's revenge would be creative—and certain.

At lunchtime, he chose a table off by himself and faced the wall.

"This looks like an interesting table. Let's sit here, girls." Gwenny placed her tray next to Rudy's left elbow. Colleen and Jennifer wiggled into the seats facing him. Shandra plunked herself down on Rudy's right, and Kim squeezed in beside her.

Here it comes, thought Rudy.

"I got the cutest top at the mall last night," Colleen said.

"What's it look like?" asked Jennifer.

"It's pale blue—a soft, baby blue—and has these darling little ruffles around the neck and around the sleeves."

"I think I saw it," cried Shandra, leaning across Rudy's tray.

He rescued his applesauce dish.

"Does it have teensy-weensy birdies down one side?"

"That's it! I'm going to wear it to my sister's seventh-grade barbecue on Sunday."

Rudy almost pinched himself to make sure he wasn't invisible.

"Speaking of the mall," Gwenny said, "I saw these earrings I really want. They have three gold rings with a red heart on top. Ultra-ultra romantic."

Kim squealed.

Rudy squirmed with embarrassment.

The girls leaned across Rudy and began to compare earrings. "When are you getting your ears pierced, Kim?"

"My father says I can do it on my birthday—that's in January—and you can all go with me and help me pick out a whole wardrobe of earrings."

"Start with birthstone earrings. January is garnets. Deep red. You'll look gorgeous!"

"The other day I saw the cutest little white snowflakes," Colleen said.

"You'll need some long, dangling earrings for special occasions." Jennifer shook her head back and forth. "Then every time you toss your head, you can feel your earrings bouncing against your neck."

"Maybe I'll have an earring sleepover on my birthday."

"We'll all bring our earrings and . . ."

Rudy's head swiveled from one speaker to the next. Nasty remarks he could handle—but girl talk?

"Have you seen the latest issue of *Smarty*?"

Gwenny asked. "There's this new hairstyle out that's guaranteed to drive boys wild." The girls shrieked.

Rudy shrank into himself and tried to tune them out. Apparently, Gwenny hadn't told them she'd been stood up. She wasn't through with him. Not by a long shot.

Dinner tonight promised to explode like a hand grenade. And he had pulled the pin.

*   *   *   *   *

"So you're the famous Rudy Benson. Gwenny's been telling me about you for weeks."

Rudy's mind careened through the possibilities: his pitching ability? his acting crazy in class? his astute comments in youth group?

Clyde patted the sofa. "Have a seat," he invited. "Plaster statues can't move around much."

"Does it hurt?" Rudy asked. The cast looked like a stuffed athletic sock encasing Clyde's leg from thigh to ankle.

"Not any more, but it sure slaughtered my game this season. Guess it was a blessing in disguise, though. I started taking some college classes in case this knee sidelines me permanently. That's where I met Margaret—in a music theory class."

"You're a musician?"

"Yep. I play a mean jazz clarinet. Also write music in my spare time. Baseball isn't a lifetime job, so I'd better have something else going for me. I'm heading for a Masters in music education."

Clyde Reilly, first baseman for the Clinton Pilots, wasn't trying for the majors? Didn't all players want to make the majors?

"Tell me about the Seventh Street Sluggers. I hear you built the team from the ground up. Quite a success story."

After that, it was easy. Words spilled out of Rudy's mouth like water over a waterfall. He must have asked a hundred questions before his parents arrived.

Mom disappeared into the kitchen, and Dad clattered down to Doctor Mac's basement workshop.

Margaret, Gwenny's sister, came into the room just as Rudy was asking Clyde what he thought about the Series. "Hi, Rudy. Good to see you." Her welcoming smile showed in her eyes as well as on her lips. "Gwenny talks about you constantly."

"What does she say?" Rudy blurted out.

"All sorts of things." Margaret winked. "It wouldn't be fair if I told you."

"Dinner's ready." Margaret placed a gentle kiss on Clyde's cheek. Her hair, darker than Gwenny's, fanned out around her face like soft butterfly wings.

Dad and Dr. Mac emerged from his basement workshop. Margaret and Mrs. Mac started serving dinner. Gwenny slipped silently into her chair and stared down at her plate.

"I'm practicing my cooking on you," announced Mrs. Mac proudly. "Last week, I graduated from a World Brotherhood cooking class."

She started a parade of serving dishes around the table. Rudy eyed the first bowl warily. Little lumps crouched in its depths like rodents in green slime. His father cleared his throat. Rudy scooped a wrinkled mound onto his plate and quickly handed the dish to Margaret.

"I couldn't believe some of the ingredients," she said. "I'm determined to develop a strong stomach before I go with the outreach team next summer."

Clyde laughed as he plopped gray mush on his plate. "Those black things you brought me the other night—I hadn't a clue until I bit through the skin. What a surprise!"

Rudy breathed through his mouth and doggedly served himself something that resembled dog food. Disgusting pictures surged through his mind.

"Witchitty grubs," Gwenny said darkly. "They eat them in Australia."

Clyde handed Rudy a bowl of pink globs floating in blood red sauce.

"Rat hearts," Gwenny said distinctly. "No matter what you cover them up with, they're still rat hearts."

"Gwenny!" Mrs. Mac snapped. "I do *not* cook rats. Everything here is quite acceptable."

"Rudy knows all about rat hearts."

"Things aren't always the way they look," he said defensively.

"That's for sure," Dr. Mac said. "One winter we took in an old woman who lived under a bridge. Carried an ax for protection. Once the dirt came off, we found she had six grandkids and a heart as sweet as pie."

"Sometimes it works the other way," Gwenny said. "Sometimes you really trust someone—and find out that person is rotten inside."

"Maybe there's good inside, but nobody sees it," Rudy shot back.

"A rat is a rat is a rat."

"Hey," said Dr. Mac. "Remember? 'Man looks at the outward appearance, but the Lord looks at the heart.'"

Rudy cut into a little corpse. Tiny bones grated against his knife. He sighed with relief. At least it wasn't an insect.

After dinner, Dr. Mac and Rudy's dad disappeared into the basement again. Gwenny stalked into the kitchen. Over the clatter of dishes, Rudy heard Mrs. Mac say, "Gwenny, I thought you'd like to entertain Rudy."

Rudy sat on the floor beside Clyde's footstool. The food hadn't been half bad, he realized, but the pain in his innards came from another source. He folded his arms over his stomach and closed his eyes.

"I don't think it's the food that's eating you,"

observed Clyde. "You look like I feel when I put everything I have and then some into the game—and all the crowd sees is that the team lost by one run."

Rudy gulped. "That's what's happened to me."

Clyde's friendly gray eyes offered an invitation. Rudy poured out the whole story: his rotten reputation at school, the ultimatum, struggling to become the perfect student while his marvelous, terrible teeth broadcast the World Series.

"So the whole team hates me and my best friend isn't speaking to me and tomorrow at noon there's this big conference where they're going to decide that I need another year in sixth grade. Nobody sees the good—just the bad. And no matter how hard I try, it only gets worse."

Clyde nodded sympathetically. "What about —"

But Rudy, looking up from the floor, caught a glimpse of Gwenny's skirt in the darkened hall that led to the kitchen.

Gwenny, who hadn't exacted her revenge yet, now knew his deepest secret.

Panic welled up. Rudy could hardly breathe. "I've got to go," he gasped, bolting for the door.

He raced down the dark street toward home like prey seeking shelter. The wind-tossed trees created shadowy fingers that reached for him as he ran. No escape seemed possible. He was dead meat.

Chapter 9

Sunshine flooded the sky, reflecting the glow in Rudy's heart as he loped toward the school, a bulging shoe box under one arm. The Plan had appeared like a video in his mind while he brushed his teeth last night.

He saw himself, a master lawyer in a courtroom drama—pacing back and forth, waving his arms like magic wands as he molded the minds of his listeners with his superb showmanship.

He pulled exhibits from his evidence box: breeding records, math papers, *Treasure Island*, in case Ms. Throckmeir still hadn't read his extra credit report. *Finally, as the jury leaned forward, he, Home Run Rudy, made his death-defying, stunningly spectacular move and .*

He yanked open the school door and stepped inside.

Mr. Spinelli, a red Ping-Pong ball tied over his nose, struggled to fill the many pockets on his clown suit with toys. A sign sprouted under his bow tie:

"one ticket = one pick."

"Talk about perfect timing! Can you do my back pockets?"

Rudy stuffed a dozen pockets on the back of the costume with little kid stuff: plastic bracelets, stickers, crazy erasers, and black rubber spiders. "You won't be able to sit down all day," he joked.

A flash of white caught his attention. Morton looked like a waiter as he flipped sheets over tables that lined the hall.

"Hey, Morton! Who won the pool yesterday?"

Morton didn't answer. He turned his back. Rudy swallowed hard.

"Somebody—help!" a familiar voice shouted. Rudy swung around. Charlie's face peered over a gigantic coconut cake dotted with maraschino cherries. His tray slanted left, then right, the cake sliding from one edge to the other. He lurched down the hall, trying to compensate.

"Got it." Rudy's thumbs plowed through frosting as he grabbed the runaway cake and placed it on the sale table beside a chocolate, computer-shaped creation sporting a keyboard of red icing dots.

He sucked his thumbs. Quickly, he repaired the cake by smearing over the gouges his thumbs had made. A couple of rubs netted him another tongue-full of frosting. He eyed Charlie warily.

"Who won?"

"Rusty won the pool yesterday," Charlie said flatly.

His eyes glittered with anger.

"You remember what happens to me at noon?"

Charlie shrugged and looked away.

Screech! Squawk! The sounds pierced Rudy's ears like fingernails on a chalkboard. He peered into the gym. Ms. Throckmeir, wearing blue jeans, struggled with a wooden backboard for the beanbag toss.

"Wait!" Rudy yelled. He charged over to help. Together they wrestled the huge plywood target against a wall. Sweat trickled down Ms. Throckmeir's temples, and she removed her glasses to wipe her face with her shirt sleeve.

"Thanks, Rudy," she gasped. For a moment, a curtain parted in Rudy's mind and he could almost imagine his teacher filling her gas tank, shopping at the supermarket, going to church—things his own mom did. Then reason returned.

"I'll set up the chairs," Rudy announced, heading toward the janitor's closet. Lugging metal folding chairs around to the booths and setting them up for the cakewalk was noisy and noticeable. Also, hard work. Something she would remember.

He sneaked a glance over his shoulder as he banged the chairs into place. Where was Gwenny? She always stood out in a crowd like some sort of celebrity.

Charlie and Rusty sauntered past him toward the makeup table.

"Hey, guys," Rudy called. "Where's Gwenny?"

No answer. The boys kept on walking.

"How 'bout a new look, Charlie?" Shandra squealed, shaking a bunch of makeup brushes. She tilted her head and made cow eyes at him.

"Go paint yourself green!" Charlie laughed.

Rudy wiped sweaty hands on his jeans. He felt a prickle behind his eyes.

"Dumb allergy," he mumbled to himself.

Girls clustered around the makeup table, lining up lipsticks and strange little pots and bottles. Three standing mirrors reflected their laughing faces.

No Gwenny.

Rudy doubted if death itself could keep her away from a makeup table. He remembered her angry face from last night. Her words sharp as swords.

Goose bumps popped out on his arms.

By eleven o'clock, people packed the school, jabbering above the beat of intercom music, munching hot dogs and trying their luck at the games. Scents of buttered popcorn and cotton candy filled the air. Mr. Anderson, dressed like a cowboy, hunched over a table by the front door.

"Step right up, folks. Buy twenty tickets and get two free."

He ripped off strips of pink tickets and stashed money in an old fishing tackle box.

Everywhere Rudy went, a glassy-eyed school clock mocked him, its second hand sweeping away the time before his conference. He had stashed his shoe box of evidence inside the office, but his brain felt like the gray mush he'd eaten last night. He couldn't remember his brilliant defense speech. Action. Anything to occupy his mind.

"Ms. Throckmeir? Let me open those ice cream boxes."

"I'll get the extra tickets out of your van, Mr. Anderson."

"Sure, I'll blow up more balloons, Mr. Spinelli."

Rudy worked like a starving animal performing for food. Tucked in his belt, his own strip of pink tickets fluttered as he raced from job to job. His stomach growled fiercely, but he couldn't stop for food.

He spotted Gwenny at 11:20. She was dancing up and down, waving her hands and talking earnestly with Mr. Alvarez. In the center of the gym stood a gold-wrapped table. It held a stack of plastic bowls, empty glass jars with labels and a bright aluminum pot filled with glossy, boiled eggs. Purple signs with silver sparkles announced: "Special Contest: Bites for Bytes" and "Cheer on Your Favorite Contestant: two tickets per egg."

"Hear ye, hear ye!" Gwenny's voice rang out over the microphone.

Conversation stopped.

"Today, we have a surprise contest to raise more money for our school computers. Ladies and gentlemen, boys and girls—we're here to pick Elmwood's first chow champion! Students will compete to see who can eat the most hard-boiled eggs—and collect the most tickets."

"Yea," cried some of the younger kids.

"Choose your contestant. At the end of each round, you put a ticket in their jar for every egg they ate. The one with the most tickets will be crowned Elmwood's Computer King—or Queen!"

"Eight people have already signed up." Gwenny read some third and fourth grade names into the microphone.

"The fifth grade contestants are Vinnie Starbuck and Carla Webb."

"Representing Mr. Anderson's sixth grade class, we have Antonio Garcia. From Ms. Throckmeir's class: Morton Fleever . . . "

"I'll put my tickets on Morton Fleever," Rudy shouted. "He can really pack it away!"

"I'm afraid you can't do that," Gwenny shot back. "The other person from Ms. Throckmeir's class is *you!*"

"No way." Rudy shook his head and grinned. "I've got a conference at noon."

"You've got plenty of time, Rudy. Let's see how many tickets you can sell for our new computers! What do you say, everybody?"

"We want Ru-dee! We want Ru-dee!" the sixth-graders chanted.

He eyed the crowd. Ms. Throckmeir smiled. Mr. Spinelli shook his fist in the air to cheer him on.

The yelling intensified. Now, the crowd clapped in rhythm. *Clap! Clap! "We want Ru-dee! We want Ru-dee!"*

"Okay! Okay! You've got me!" Rudy lifted his hands in surrender.

The contestants from each grade squared off on folding chairs around the table. Gwenny set a bowl of six peeled eggs and a glass of water in front of each one along with a jar marked "Tickets." Six glistening eyeballs stared up at Rudy. His throat felt funny. If he threw up now, he was lost.

Mind over matter, he told himself. *Pretend they're scoops of ice cream.*

"You have five minutes to complete the first round," Gwenny explained. If you haven't eaten all of your eggs, you're out of the contest. We'll pass your ticket jars at the end of each session, and you decide if you can keep going."

Mr. Spinelli took the mike. "These kids need your support," he boomed. "Cheer them on. Let's hear it for Elmwood's Chow Champion!"

Whistles and shouts filled the air.

"Ready—set—go!"

Rudy winced as he bit into the first rubbery egg. It smelled like the time the sewer had backed up in his basement. He swigged a bit of water—just enough to get the egg down. *Don't fill up on water*, he cautioned himself.

Morton stuck his skinny neck over the table like

one of the flamingos at the zoo—the kind that eat fish whole. Instantly, Rudy saw a clear path from the table to the championship. He balanced the second egg delicately between his thumb and second finger, maneuvering it so that the narrow end pointed down. He stretched his neck up like a shore bird— the way he did when Dr. Graham poked a wooden tongue depressor against his tongue and told him to say, "Ahh."

Quick as a fish, the shiny egg glided down.

Once, he'd accidentally swallowed a whole ice cube. He'd forgotten about the ache that paralyzed his chest. The cold egg worked the same way. Water eased the pain a little.

"All right! Let's hear it for Rudy," Gwenny screamed.

Rudy eyed the next egg. Slimy. *Think fish. Think fish.* He opened his throat and the egg slithered down.

Two younger kids left the table early.

"Give 'em a hand for a good try," Gwenny yelled.

Another egg. More pain. Finally, the timer dinged.

Kids tossed tickets into their contestant's jars. More contestants disappeared into the crowd, and Gwenny set up the second round.

It was down to Vinnie, Carla, Morton, and Rudy.

Six white eggs formed a damp pyramid. Rudy sipped the water and let it trickle slowly down, moistening the edges of his throat.

"Ready, set, go!"

He closed his eyes. He imagined the warm air ruffling his feathers. He concentrated on the feel of chill water between his long, scaly toes. Another egg slid down his throat.

He glanced around the table. Vinnie took forever to chew his egg. He swigged down enough water to wallow in before reaching for the next one.

Morton chewed like a cow—sort of a side-to-side motion. Rudy snorted and popped in his next to last egg.

Morton's cheeks pooched out chipmunk style. He stared into space, chewing, chewing . . .

Carla suddenly bolted away from the table.

Burp! Vinnie belched as he finished his last egg.

The audience went wild.

"Win, Vin, win! Win, Vin, win!" they shouted.

"Morton Fleever, big achiever! Morton Fleever . . . "

"Go! Ru-dee, go! Go! Ru-dee go!"

Morton's face turned a blotchy green and white. *Crash!* He knocked over his chair and charged toward the hall.

Round three. Sixth versus fifth. A matter of face, now.

Rudy's stomach churned.

"Vinnie! Vinnie!" the crowd yelled.

"Ru-dee! Ru-dee!"

Gwenny smacked the two bowls down. "You need to *chew* this round, Rudy. Trust me," she whispered.

Faintly, her words registered.

Maybe the chewed parts would filter between the whole eggs and take up less space. That made sense. Up and down, up and down. Rudy's jaws moved in time with the chanting.

Another egg.

Thick, gummy paste plastered his braces. Only water moved the sludge down his throat. Time lost all meaning. His mind felt suspended. He seemed to be watching from the ceiling—looking down on two boys doggedly eating while the crowd went crazy.

Fourth round.

Rudy chewed on auto pilot. Dimly, he saw Vinnie shake his head.

Then a horrible sound split his consciousness.

The noon bell rang!

Chapter

10

Ker-chunk. Mr. Alvarez closed the door to his inner office. It sounded to Rudy like a prison gate slamming shut. Sounds of the carnival disappeared. The adults took their places around the conference table, and Rudy folded himself into a chair. He squirmed to find a position that didn't strain his bloated belly. The shoe box of exhibits sat on the table in front of him.

It was thought control that counted now. Forget his stomach. Forget the ringing in his ears. Concentrate on remembering The Plan.

"Mr. and Mrs. Benson, I'd like you to meet Dr. Yasuzawa, our school superintendent," Mr. Alvarez said. Gravely, Dr. Yasuzawa shook their hands.

"I know I don't have to tell any of you about the importance of this conference," he said. "Having observed him in the classroom, I take a particular interest in your son's case."

Mr. Alvarez removed some papers from a folder. "Rudy, you've had a week to consider your situation.

Have you given serious thought to the possibility of remaining at Elmwood Elementary for another year?"

"Yes, sir."

"Have you improved your work habits since we last met?"

"Yes, sir, I have."

"Let's begin by sharing what each of us has observed."

Mr. Alvarez described Rudy's hamster report. "A fine piece of work."

Rudy grinned inwardly. The graded report lay folded in his evidence box with a bright red "A" on the first page.

"If only he hadn't left school without permission in order to retrieve it."

You wouldn't have given me permission, thought Rudy.

Ms. Throckmeir pursed her lips. "He turned in all of his assignments this past week," she said. "He also did an extra-credit report on a difficult book."

So—she had found his orange folder.

"But," she continued, "he disrupted the entire class the day I broke my glasses. The substitute teacher said he tried to kiss Gwenny MacDonald."

Rudy's face grew hot. That's not at all what had happened. But she would see. They all would—after his presentation.

Dr. Yasuzawa cleared his throat. "Rudy worked

diligently in class the day I visited," he said, "but his mouth twitched and moved constantly. He seemed to be under great stress."

Another point he would clear up when it was his turn.

Dr. Pokeberry dug out a sheaf of papers from her attaché case. "His IQ tested high," she said, "but he showed signs of disturbance. He chewed on pencils, markers, and even a chalkboard eraser. He also drooled all over his knees. That certainly isn't normal behavior."

She stared at Mr. and Mrs. Benson with cold eyes. "How often do you feed him?" she asked.

The question sounded like something a zoo manager might ask one of his keepers.

Mom leaped to her feet. "I see that he gets three nutritious meals every day plus healthy snacks," she snapped. "Whole grain bread. Raw vegetables. Fresh fruits. Low-fat milk."

Dr. Pokeberry gasped and leaned back in her chair. Mom sat down again.

Rudy scratched his itchy eyebrows. He may have looked like a drooling idiot during the test, but at least he hadn't tuned in on the game. He'd beef up that part of his presentation—focus on his awesome willpower.

"You certainly kept him long enough," Ms. Throckmeir said. "He didn't return to class until the next morning."

Dr. Pokeberry glared at her. "I let him go at 2:15."

"Ah-ha! That was around the time all the boys in the class got a case of 'bathroom-itis,'" Ms. Throckmeir observed.

Rudy tried to speak, but his egg-caked braces locked. Funny patterns came and went in front of his eyes. He filled a paper cup at the water cooler and swished the liquid around in his mouth.

The adults' voices droned on like a background of honeybees. Good. Bad. He couldn't tell what conclusion they might come to. He forced himself to concentrate on The Plan.

Finally, the talking stopped. Everyone looked at Rudy. He could feel their eyes stabbing into him like darts. Pictures raced across his mind. A six-foot version of himself sprouting chin whiskers. Still in sixth grade. Surrounded by silly little kids. Alone.

He took a deep breath. His future lay on the line.

I need a miracle, Lord, he prayed silently. *Please help me.*

Rudy pushed in his chair and walked to the middle of the room. Facing his audience, he made his opening comment according to The Plan.

"There is something you should know," he said in a croaky voice. He sounded like a sick bullfrog. Clearing his throat, he started over.

"There is something you should know." That came out much better.

"I'm a baseball addict. Like an alcoholic. Or a

compulsive gambler. I can't help myself when the World Series is on. I can't control myself. It's like there's a monster inside."

He looked at Mom. "I really didn't have a headache last year during opening day. *I couldn't go to school and miss the first game.*"

He was vulnerable, now. No turning back.

"I put my radio under the pillow at Gram's. My team needed me."

No one moved.

He licked his lips. "Something comes over me— like a big tent that shuts out everything else. I keep thinking about players and statistics and stuff."

He scratched his neck.

"Remember how Albert Einstein thought about math and things so much his wife had to make sure he was dressed when he went outside? And *he* was a *genius*!"

Rudy paused. The silence in the room surrounded him like a wasteland. He wiped his palms on his shirt and stared at Ms. Throckmeir.

"I meant it when I said I changed after our meeting last week. Did you know I missed breakfast on Tuesday to get to school by seven? And I worked on the carnival two whole hours every morning."

Ms. Throckmeir nodded "You were quite diligent."

"I wanted to earn more computers for our school," Rudy added virtuously.

"Remember how long I worked on my hamster report, Dad? Saturday *and* Sunday? You even tried to get me to take a break."

Dad nodded. "I remember."

"It wasn't due until Tuesday, so I forgot to take it to school. But I skipped lunch to run home and get it during lunchtime."

"You missed two meals?" Mom croaked.

"Ah ha," exclaimed Dr. Pokeberry.

"I did my homework the minute I got home— every day."

Mom smiled. "I brought you your snacks because you didn't want to waste time getting them yourself."

Rudy paced the floor like the lawyers on TV. His armpits itched. "I wrote until 2:00 A.M. on that extra-credit book report."

Ms. Throckmeir patted her folder. "No wonder it's difficult to read. You must have been exhausted."

Rudy remembered crossing a rushing creek last summer by stepping on precariously balanced rocks. One misstep and the current would sweep him away. Did she credit him for his industry or criticize him for his handwriting?

Dad frowned. "Wasn't that the night you cleaned the garage until bedtime?"

On TV, the jurors always believed whatever the lawyer said. But Rudy couldn't read anyone's reaction to his presentation. Did staying up half the night show diligence—or stupidity? Did retrieving his hamster report during lunchtime indicate responsibility—or sneakiness?

"I know what I saw in the classroom," said Mr. Yasuzawa. "Spastic contortions."

A sense of doom hung over Rudy. He could hardly breathe. It was now or never.

He raised his head, flung out his arm dramatically and began his buildup.

"What nobody knew," he said, "was that something happened when Dr. Mac filled my tooth on Monday. My teeth kept broadcasting the World Series. It was awful. I fought like mad to keep my mind on my school work. It took a lot of character to do that."

Silence.

Rudy felt hot and cold at the same moment. His fingers tingled like the blood supply had been cut off.

"You thought my folks didn't feed me," he said to Dr. Pokeberry. "I had to put things in my mouth to keep my teeth apart so I could concentrate on the test."

More silence.

He looked at Ms. Throckmeir. "When I first read my science report, my teeth kept mixing me up, so I read it again."

Her mouth opened and closed several times.

"But I don't expect you to believe me without proof," Rudy said grandly. "I'm going to demonstrate how my teeth broadcast radio programs. You'll be amazed that I overcame technology by sheer will power. That I turned into a model student in spite of temptation."

He stationed himself in front of his audience and folded his arms. Moving his mouth to the left, Rudy brought his teeth together and lifted his lips.

Nothing.

He cleared his throat and tried again.

Still nothing. His heart beat like a kettle drum. He twisted his jaw until he felt the familiar click. He pulled his lips up so high his nose wrinkled.

Rudy's wayward teeth, once so loud and unruly, sat silently in his mouth. No amount of jaw moving could coax a single sound from his new filling.

He felt violently dizzy and leaned on the back of his chair to keep from falling over.

Grim faces set in straight lines.

"You go sit on the bench outside the office," Mr. Alvarez said. "We need to talk about this."

Rudy stumbled into the hall and listened to the door close behind him. Cut off at the roots.

Everything itched. He clawed under his T-shirt, using his fingernails like a rake.

Gwenny moved over to make room for him on the bench. The carnival swirled around him like a bad dream. He writhed in a bubble of itchy torment.

"Did it work?" Gwenny asked anxiously. "My dad said the sulfur in the egg yolks would . . . "

He struggled to breathe. The air seemed like thickening Jello. He tried to answer, but his rubbery lips couldn't form the words. Faintly, he heard Gwenny shout into the office.

"Something's wrong with Rudy."

He lay on the floor, looking up at a forest of legs. Everybody yelled at everybody else.

"Look at those hives. I'd say it's an allergic reaction."

"Could it have been something he's eaten?"

"Isn't this the kid that won the egg-eating contest?"

"Eggs?" Mom's voice sounded hysterical. "Eggs?"

Gwenny burst into tears. "It's my fault. I tricked him into eating a lot of eggs. My dad said that would stop the broadcasting."

His mother screamed. "He's violently allergic to eggs. He nearly died when he was a baby."

Gwenny's shriek drowned out other voices. "I've killed him!"

A man shouted, "Call 911."

Someone dropped a blanket over Rudy's body.

The sound of sirens. Other voices. Then, the clumping of heavy shoes.

"You the mother? You can ride up front in the ambulance. Your husband can follow us in your car."

The prick of a hypodermic came as Rudy plunged into blackness.

Chapter

II

Spiders! Millions of crawly creepers! Rudy forced his swollen eyelids open. His eyes focused on a white cloth curtain around his bed. His scalp tickled. His nostrils tingled. Even his eyeballs itched.

He fought to scratch, but his wrists, wrapped in gauze, were tied to the metal bed rails.

Prickling. Tickling. Like a mass of tiny critters scurrying up and down his body.

He kicked his legs out from the sheet and stared in horror. Swollen. Piles and piles of red bumps stacked on top of each other. Screaming to be scratched.

"Eeaahh!" The sound ripped from his throat. He squirmed to rake his toenails down one shin.

Something funny about his right hand. Adhesive tape secured it to a board. His eyes bugged. The vein on the back of his hand connected to a transparent tube dripping solution from an overhead bottle.

He had an IV! Where was the needle? His stomach lurched. The needle lay inside his vein, of course. What if he moved his hand? Would his blood start pumping the other way? Draining him like a vampire?

"Eeaahh!"

"You crazy or somethin'?" A boy's voice sliced through Rudy's panic.

Two fists lifted the curtain and black eyes, curious as question marks, peered out of a dusky face. A white plaster neck collar seemed to fasten the boy's head to his shoulders.

"Pull that sucker out and they'll stick it right back in. I oughta know."

"Who . . . ?"

"Daren Stratton. Call me Dare."

Stratton. Where had he heard that name before? Rudy arched his back and tried to scrape his bottom against the sheet.

Daren stripped the curtain back on its ceiling track and punched the call button on his own bed.

"Wonder Boy's back," he called over the intercom.

"Wonder Boy?"

Daren laughed. "Here I am, watching TV, okay? The door busts open and they wheel you in. Everything goes crazy. People pack in here, yelling and crying. TV cameras all over . . . "

"TV? Wow! Wish I'd been around to see it."

"We'll pick it up on Channel Four News tonight."

Squeaky, rubber-soled footsteps. A smiley-eyed

nurse snipped through the gauze handcuffs with a stern warning not to scratch, lowered the bed rails, and disappeared.

The door opened and Rudy's parents approached his bed on tiptoe. Tears had cut through Mom's makeup, so her cheeks resembled wrinkled walnut shells. Dad's face looked gray.

"We should have told you . . . "

Mom stared at Rudy's legs and burst into tears.

"You hated eggs so much, we never thought you'd eat . . . " Dad's voice cracked.

"I can't be allergic," Rudy said. "I eat cake, meat loaf, all sorts of stuff with eggs in them."

"You can tolerate small amounts," Mom said, "but not nineteen—"

"*Twenty-one*," Rudy interrupted. "I had to win the contest to show Ms. Throckmeir how much I participate now."

Dad hauled out his handkerchief and blew his nose.

Trays rattled outside the door. "Dinner time," a voice called from the hall.

Mom pushed his hair back from his forehead with her fingers. "Don't worry about your hamsters. We'll take care of them."

Dad patted Rudy's shoulder. "Hang in there, Sport. Doctor says we can pick you up after lunch tomorrow."

A fast-moving candy striper flattened herself

against the wall as Rudy's parents backed out of the room.

Cheerfully, she zapped the boys' beds to a sitting position and pulled rubber-tired tables across their chests.

"Daren Stratton," she read from the tray card. She popped the covers off the dishes. The fragrance of fried chicken and chocolate drifted past Rudy's nose. He salivated in anticipation.

"Rudy Benson—you have the light plate." Pale broth, Jello and apple juice. Two glasses full. Rudy froze in disbelief.

"Hey, how come . . . ?" But she had disappeared.

Crunch! Daren bit through the crust of his drumstick and smacked his lips.

"Watch that Jello," he said. "Unless you're a lefty, that is. Can't think why they always put IVs in your right hand. He picked up his hot-buttered corn-on-the-cob and gestured with it. "I nearly starved before I figured out how to eat with my left hand."

Rudy bent over his broth. He'd better keep his eyes off Daren. The smell of corn made his nose twitch. Think about something else. "How many times have you been in the hospital?" he asked.

Daren slurped his chocolate milk. "Four times," he said. "Number one: when I got born. Number two: when I fell off our roof and hit my head. Number three: last year I had stitches. Number four: now."

"What happened?"

"Did a somersault off the top step in my grand-ma's house." He laughed. "My momma shipped me off to Elmwood so's to get me away from the gangs in the city. 'You'll be safe,' she said. Same day I got here, I tripped and ended up with my neck broke. I'm gonna get some shorter laces."

Rudy inspected his green Jello. A thumbprint dec-orated the top. Could he get his plastic spoon through the shimmering square?

Swoosh—splat! Jello shot through the air and plopped onto the floor.

"Nice shot. I can see the headlines: 'Wonder Boy starves to death in hospital.'" Daren licked the choco-late frosting on his cake. Little waves of chocolate welled up in front of his tongue.

Rudy gulped and turned away. He concentrated on running his fingernails down his itchy arms. Up and down.

"You at the middle school?" Anything to keep his mind off his stomach and his skin.

"Maybe next year, if I get caught up. When I get outta here, I'll be in sixth at Elmwood Elementary." Daren said.

"No kidding! You might be in my class!"

They grinned at each other.

"I'll introduce you around. Do you play base-ball?"

"Like Hank Aaron himself. My stepbrother's

cousin taught me. He plays in the minors." Daren held his fork in two hands and swung at an imaginary ball.

"Ever hear of Clyde Reilly?" Rudy asked.

"You bet. Sometimes, Boyd lets me watch practice. Clyde's terrific."

An unpleasant awareness hit Rudy. "I have to use the bathroom," he said.

Daren made a face. "You've got two choices. Ring for the nurse and ask her to help—or walk yourself into our bathroom."

"But my IV . . . "

"You've got wheels, man. Use 'em. It's easy."

Carefully, Rudy inched himself off the edge of the bed, keeping his IV hand still. Good. No blood gushed up the tube. He plodded on unsteady legs, pushing the IV stand with his left hand. He felt a breeze under the second tie on his hospital gown.

Daren snickered. "Nice underwear."

Rudy winced. He'd worn his baseball underwear this morning for luck. Bright red with black bats and white baseballs. Inside, he slammed the bathroom door. *Bang!*

He flushed the toilet a few times and played with the water in the sink. Had he made a fool of himself today? Did anybody at school see his lucky underpants? It was scary to know that hundreds of onlookers had watched him after he'd passed out.

He peered into the mirror. Blotches of red—

lumpy lips. Is that what he looked like in front of the whole school?

Finally, he opened the door. Daren stood a foot away.

"Someone's here to see you," he whispered. "In the sun room. I'll show you where."

Rudy grabbed the back of his hospital gown with his left hand and pushed the IV stand with his right forearm. Awkwardly, he shuffled behind Daren. They made a right. Then another.

"Through there." Daren pointed.

Rudy entered a dimly-lit room with a glass ceiling. Trees and other large plants grew in orange pots. They formed little oases around soft, vinyl chairs and plastic coffee tables. In one corner, an old couple held hands and drank soda pop from aluminum cans.

"Rudy—over here." A small figure in a blue bathrobe peered over the back of a tree-draped chair. Even across the room, Rudy could make out the dandelion-gone-to-seed hair. Gwenny.

"What's . . . ? What are you doing here?" he stammered. He sank carefully into the next chair.

"Pretending to be a patient." She pulled at the neck of her robe and handed him a homemade envelope. He unfolded a large pink heart covered with writing. Even through the shadows, Rudy could make out the words, "I'm Sorry," written hundreds of times. Up, down, around, and through the center of the paper. Each one in a different color. Some sparkled with glitter.

Gwenny closed her eyes. "After you went home last night, I talked to my dad. He told me chewing egg yolks would stop the broadcasting in your teeth. So, I tried to help by—"

"Setting up the egg-eating contest?"

"Right. Only I didn't know you were allergic."

"Me, neither," said Rudy. They sat staring at each other, Rudy's eyes swollen and itchy, Gwenny's filled with tears.

"I'd better go before someone discovers I'm missing," said Rudy.

"Me, too. My ride's in the parking lot."

Gwenny scurried out the nearest door.

Excited voices spilled down the hallway. Clyde lay on Rudy's bed, leaning back on one elbow, resting his cast on top of the covers. Baseball cards covered both table tops.

"Here's our hero," Clyde said, grinning. "You look ghastly."

"Gee, thanks!"

"You gotta pay your dues if you're gonna be Wonder Boy," said Daren.

Neatly, Clyde slid off the bed and waved toward the tables. "Guess you guys can divvy these up. I have a lady waiting for me in the parking lot." The thud of his cast grew faint as he stumped down the hall.

"Wow!" Daren exploded. "Boyd's never introduced me to Clyde Reilly." He gazed at his right hand. "I'm not gonna wash this dude for a week!"

"I already have Tim McCarver," Rudy said, pawing through the cards. "How about you taking him?"

"Okay. Then I get next pick."

They tuned in to the TV news early and waited through three car ads, a long distance phone pitch, and a commercial for a home equity loan. Finally, Bill Peterson appeared on the screen. He reported the latest crimes, accidents, and court battles.

"They oughta call this the 'bad news' program," Daren grumbled.

Rudy held his breath and waited. For all the hoopla he'd gotten, his story definitely wasn't headline news.

After the third round of commercials, the camera zoomed in on Bill Peterson's face. "On a brighter note, here's the story of a hometown boy who scored a winning run today. A lesson for all of us."

The picture switched to a crowd scene. Police officers and fire fighters crouched around something— someone—only the blue-jeaned legs showed. Ms. Throckmeir clung to Dr. Pokeberry. Tears ran down their cheeks.

"Turn up the sound," Rudy said.

"Sixth-grader, Rudy Benson, put his life on the line today, to prove to Elmwood Elementary School authorities that he'd changed from class clown to serious student in the period of one week."

Pictures flashed on the screen. Rescue workers obscured Rudy—except for his legs. A pack of students stood in the background, mouths open like astonished fish.

Come on. Show my face.

"Young Benson, an avid baseball fan, collapsed at a school fund-raising contest, after swallowing twenty-one eggs, to which he is violently allergic. School authorities had earmarked the proceeds to finance an updated computer laboratory. This earnest young man exemplifies the ideal student, devoted to bettering his school."

"Hot dog!" Daren yelled. "You got guts all right!"

Paramedics formed a wall beside a rolling stretcher. The camera zoomed in on Mr. Alvarez, his lower teeth gnawing on his moustache.

"In recognition of Benson's courage, Channel Four has set up a fund in his name. All proceeds will go to purchase computers and software. Call in your pledge tonight. Let's show Rudy Benson the people of Elmwood are behind him in his efforts to improve the level of education for all youngsters."

The cameras recorded an ambulance backing up to the emergency room door. Medical workers pushed a blanket-covered mound into the hospital.

Show my face, Rudy screamed inwardly.

Daren's face flashed on the screen, complete with wide eyes and his plaster neck collar. He smiled at the camera.

On came an old photo of Rudy as a first grader, with four front teeth missing.

"We're happy to report that Rudy is recovering nicely at Elmwood Hospital."

The news anchor's face faded into a picture of the White House. Rudy flipped the switch.

"Whoopee!" he yelled. "I'm famous! A hero! A TV star!"

Chapter

12

"You gonna sleep all day?"

Rudy opened his eyes and saw Daren returning from the bathroom.

"My doctor came in early. I get to go home."

"You're leaving?"

"Yep. I'll be lugging this collar around for a while, but the doc says he's gonna kick me outta here. Grandma Birdie's comin' soon as she gets her breakfast." He chuckled. "My grandma never misses a meal for any*thing* or any*body*."

Rudy stretched. His legs didn't itch. His lips felt normal. Except for a few bumps on his chest, the hives seemed to have disappeared.

Daren leaned closer. "Your eyes are blue. Yesterday, your eyelids puffed up so much I couldn't tell."

Rudy's awakening seemed to bring on a burst of activity. The nurse made her rounds, a resident doctor stopped in with orders to remove the IV, and breakfast appeared.

This morning, gray mush (oatmeal) tasted so good Rudy asked for seconds.

Fruit. Bacon. Toast with jelly. He wolfed it down and drank two cartons of chocolate milk.

"Grandma Birdie's got a one-track mind—making something outta me," said Daren. "President, she'd go for. Maybe a famous surgeon, someone who transplants hearts. Or a doctor who develops a cure for some disease."

By the time Daren had pulled on jeans and a T-shirt, his grandmother walked through the door.

"Grandma Birdie" fit her to a tee. She looked like a small ball on bird legs. Her white hair stuck out from the sides of her wrinkled face, framing the small gold-rimmed spectacles that rested on her nose.

"You gonna tie those laces or should I do it?" She started toward Daren's bed, but he grinned and pulled his foot up on the mattress and tied his own athletic shoes.

"Come on, Grandma Birdie. I'm not gonna break anything."

She turned to Rudy. "I watched you on TV last night. Or heard about you, anyway. What with all those doctors and Daren waving at the camera, I didn't get a look at your face. Pleased to meet you. Do you go to church, young man?"

"Yes, ma'am. First Street Church."

"Every week?"

"Every Sunday and most Wednesday nights. And sometimes our youth group meets to—"

"Daren's new to town," she interrupted. She winked at him. "I'm going to make sure he gets in with the right crowd this time.

"Don't just stand there, Daren. Let's get moving. You start school tomorrow. You'll probably see our hero there one of these days."

Daren gave Rudy a thumbs-up as they left. "See you around," he said.

The minutes passed like hours. Rudy kept glancing at the second hand on his watch to be sure it was still working.

The Series should be coming on pretty soon. As he waited, Rudy thought about the past week.

Last Sunday, after church, he'd labored over his hamster report. He still had friends. Nobody thought he was crazy. He had never heard of broadcasting teeth. Life seemed simple then. Work hard, clear your name, and everything would turn out all right.

On the other hand, he now had a friend in the minors, Gwenny didn't bug him anymore, he'd survived the allergy attack, and he had made the evening news!

Dr. Mac always said that God works in mysterious ways. If this was a sample, he wondered what lay around the corner. Actually, he could hardly wait to find out.

*　　*　　*　　*　　*

Dad picked him up after lunch. "Mom's manning the phones," he told Rudy.

"Phones?"

"A figure of speech. At least fifty people called after the news last night. Mr. Alvarez phoned this morning. So much money is coming into the 'Rudy Benson Computer Fund,' he's talking about a fully-equipped lab built as an addition to the school."

Rudy flexed his muscles. "Wonder Boy strikes again!" he shouted.

*　　*　　*　　*　　*

"Surprise!"

Rudy stood inside his front door and heard the living room explode with cheers and whistles.

Crepe paper streamers hung from the ceiling. Kids popped out from their hiding places behind the drapes and furniture. It looked like his entire Sunday School class. He counted noses. Only Gwenny's was missing.

"Welcome home!" Dr. Mac's smile stretched across his face like an ad for his own dentistry. He grabbed Rudy by the hand and pulled him into the center of the room.

"Since you couldn't make church today, we

decided to come to you!" With a dramatic bow, he offered Rudy the most comfortable chair.

"Kids," he said, "here's a living example of answered prayer."

Cheers. Eddie's whistle shrilled through the noise.

"Grab a seat, everybody. We need to talk. Some things have changed since we last met," Dr. Mac said.

Kevin sat on the floor with Eddie. Kim Yang perched on the arm of Shandra's chair.

"We have bad news and good news. The bad news is that Yang's Paint Company refused to sell us the paint we need for painting the house in Lost Hill next month."

Groans.

"The good news is that Kim's dad is *donating* all the paint we need."

"All right!" yelled Kevin. Shandra hugged Kim. Some of the guys exchanged high fives.

"I'm also glad to report that every one of you has saved up enough money to make the trip. Some of you washed cars, others mowed lawns, took care of people's pets, and baby-sat. You worked hard."

Rudy sighed with relief. It had been a close call for some of the kids, especially for Eddie. His dad had died the year before.

"Now, we have quite a bit of money to consider. I want you to think about putting it to good use."

"Paint another house."

"Let's buy Christmas presents for poor children."

"No! Save it for our missions trip in the spring."

Dr. Mac held up his hands. "Hold on," he protested. "I said to think about it. Let's not make a snap
decision on something this important."

He glanced out the window. "Ah, right on time.
Sit tight, kids. We have company coming."

The doorbell rang. Everyone looked at Rudy. He
heaved himself out of his chair and opened the door.

On the porch stood Gwenny and the rest of the
Seventh Street Sluggers. Clyde and Margaret waited
with them, jingling their car keys.

Morton stared straight ahead and went into his
robot routine. "Earthling, we come in peace, bearing
gifts."

"He's in shock." Charlie laughed. "You gonna
stand there all day or do we get to come in?"

"Hey, guys!" called Eddie from his place on the
floor.

Rudy's teammates filed in with their hands
behind their backs and stood around the wall while
Gwenny introduced them to the youth group.

"And now," Dr. Mac said, "your friends have a
surprise for you."

Rusty shuffled his feet and looked embarrassed.
"We . . . we want you to have everything that was in
the jackpot Friday."

Morton went first. He held a little box out to
Rudy. Inside lay a butterfly with spread wings. "It's a
'painted lady.' One of my best."

Rudy held the box up to the window. A shaft of sunlight caught the orange and black pattern on the wings, and the colors seemed to shimmer.

Tony spoke up. "If the weather's okay next Friday night, you want to bring your sleeping bag and camp out in my backyard?"

"Sure!" Rudy said.

"Here," said Kevin, rising from his spot beside Eddie. He carefully laid a stamp on Rudy's palm. "Florida Everglades, 1948. I've got some stamp hinges in my pocket if you need one."

Rudy looked down at a picture of a white bird against a green map of Florida.

"Eddie? It's your turn."

He crawled behind the sofa and came out with a covered aquarium. Setting it down on the floor in front of Rudy's chair, he whipped off the towel. Two sleek snakes coiled in gleaming loops, their tongues flickering in and out, seeking information.

"Wow." Rudy dropped to his knees. "How long can I keep them?"

"One month from today," Eddie said grandly. "I'll fill you in on how to care for them later."

Finally, Charlie brought out a file card. He read aloud: "One month of Saturday chores by Charlie Freeman." He grinned. "Your chores are gonna be a picnic compared with Eddie's!" He looked at Rudy with steady eyes.

Rudy drew a shaky breath. His heart leaped.

Charlie, his best friend. Good old Charlie was back!

Morton and Rusty shuffled their feet. Tony folded his arms and cleared his throat. For the first time, two important groups in Rudy's life—his teammates and his church friends were meeting.

"Hear ye, hear ye." Gwenny's voice shrilled. Rudy's mind snapped back to the last time he'd heard those terrible words. To the gym. To the egg-eating contest. He shivered.

"We're going to have an egg hunt, everybody. Just follow the directions on the egg I give you and don't let anyone else see."

She handed a white paper egg to each person.

"Your instructions are top secret," Gwenny ordered. "An automatic out for anyone who talks."

Rudy looked at his paper. Gwenny's neat cursive said, "Under the upstairs telephone."

"On your mark, get set, *go!*"

Silent chaos. The kids wove in and out, each intent on following the directions. Kim headed for the kitchen; Rusty charged out the front door; Shandra started for the basement.

Rudy took the stairs two at a time, raced to the end of the hall and looked under the phone on his dad's nightstand. Another paper egg stared up at him.

"Basement. Behind the pickled beets."

He plunged down the stairs, through the kitchen, and started to the basement.

Another egg. "On the back of your kitchen curtain."

He yanked the tape off and read, "Under the pink violet in the living room."

At first, it was hard to work his way through the mass of kids. Twice, he opened his mouth to say something, but remembered to clamp his lips together before any sound leaked out. After a few minutes, most of the kids had disappeared. Where was everybody? Doggedly, Rudy hunted down each egg and followed its directions.

Finally, as he grabbed the egg under the mat in the bathroom, he realized how quiet the house had grown. Was he the only person still playing?

The egg read: "Your dad's tool bench."

He flung open the door to the garage and skidded to a stop. The kids were sitting silently around a Ping-Pong table, their hands clamped over their mouths. Rudy could see Morton's giant grin extending beyond his fingers.

"Slowpoke!" they yelled in unison.

The table was packed with food. Pizza. Bread sticks. Hot dogs. Chips. Caramel corn. Bowls of fresh fruit. In the center sat an enormous cake. Rudy read the iced inscription in amazement: "To Home Run Rudy from Ms. Throckmeir." There was even a bat and ball outlined in icing.

"She guarantees it's egg free," Mom said, coming up behind him.

Gwenny shoved a paper plate into his hands. "Better hurry," she warned. "We're starving and *you* are in our way."

Everyone talked at once. Members of the youth group sat with Seventh Street Sluggers. Morton's fists punched the air as he talked. Charlie crammed pizza in his mouth and laughed at something Shandra said.

In twenty minutes, the only proof of their party lay in crumbs on the platters and a pile of paper plates in the trash.

Dr. Mac stood and gave a piercing whistle. "Everybody back to the living room for today's lesson," he called.

They crowded into the living room, sharing the chairs, sitting on the stairs, lying on the floor. Rudy stretched out on the carpet. He'd expected the Sluggers to sit off by themselves, but he had to look through the entire group to find each one. Rusty, Tony, Charlie, and Morton all laughed and talked as though they'd known the youth group kids all their lives.

"Well, gang," Dr. Mac said, "this has been quite a week. Our Scripture for October, 'Man looks at the outward appearance, but the Lord looks at the heart' isn't any easy one. Who put it into practice?"

Hands shot up.

"Kim?"

"The crabby old lady next door used to scare me. Then I noticed how gentle she is with her dogs and decided to give her another chance. Now, she's teaching me how to train my puppy."

"Sounds good. Rudy?"

Everyone quieted down when Rudy stood up and flashed his hospital bracelet. "Did everybody see the news on TV? About how I risked my life to raise money for our computer room?"

"Yeah!"

"We knew you could do it!"

"I want you to know it wasn't true. I entered the egg contest because I wanted to show Ms. Throckmeir and Mr. Alvarez I had cut out the silly stuff and that I had changed. I guess everybody here knows about my broadcasting teeth and the problems they caused. The bottom line is, I didn't want to spend another year in sixth grade. But they didn't believe me after I ate the eggs because my teeth stopped broadcasting."

"Thanks for your honesty," Dr. Mac said.

The doorbell rang.

"I'll get it," Gwenny said.

A familiar voice drifted in like rapid little bird chirps. "Is this Rudy Benson's house? You in the youth group? Well, I finally tracked you down. My grandson, Daren Stratton, is supposed to . . . "

Rudy leaped out of his chair as Daren and Grandma Birdie stepped into the room. Daren's arms held four small cartons. Grandma Birdie's fingers clutched a sheet of yellow paper.

"So you're the D. Stratton we've been expecting," Dr. Mac said. The note I got was written so sloppily, I thought it said 'Darlene.'"

Rudy clapped his hand to his forehead. "I never made the connection."

Daren and Rudy started to laugh. Soon everyone was howling and slapping their knees. Grandma Birdie's laugh twittered high above the others.

"I almost forgot," she said, handing Rudy the yellow paper.

He scanned the note. "Listen to this, gang."

To my favorite scientist: Here are some additions to your hamster family. I hope you will stop in to talk about your breeding program when you're in middle school next year. Sincerely, Mr. Alvarez.

"Whoopee!" Rudy shouted.

"These are for you," Daren said, when the kids quieted down. "A man with a moustache asked me to bring them in."

Daren started across the living room with the stack of little cartons, but his plaster collar kept him from seeing the floor.

"Yow!" he yelled, tripping over Rusty's foot. The boxes tumbled to the carpet. Out burst four terrified hamsters. They took off in different directions.

"Quick," yelled Rudy. He and Gwenny dived for the largest hamster as it zipped under the sofa.

Crash! They collided in midair and bounced off each other like bowling pins.

Rudy took a nose dive into the end table. When he stood up, a tiny trickle of blood ran from the corner of his mouth, and he held a bracket from his metal braces in his palm.

He sighed and looked at Doctor Mac. "Looks like I need another Monday morning appointment," he said.

Doctor Mac took a look and grinned. "Cheer up," he joked. "A new bracket means you can start broadcasting again!"

Gwenny gasped.

It took only a moment for Rudy to recover. "You bet." He faded back, cocked his arm and threw for the end zone.

"I'll be set for the football playoffs!"

The End

Look for these and other exciting products from ChariotVictor...

D.J. Dillion Series
by Lee Roddy

Great action and God's values accompany D.J. on his many adventures that readers ages 8-12 will be sure to enjoy. Retail: $4.99 each

Accidental Detectives Mysteries
by Sigmund Brower

Follow Ricky, his troublesome little brother Joel, Lisa,
and the gang as they face unexpected adventures
and have to use the wisdom and strength
God gave them to get out of some tight spots.
An exciting series for 8-12 year olds.
Retail: $4.99 each

Truth Quest Series
by Tad Hardy

Rachel and her cousin Elliot encounter mysterious
people and discover many exciting things as they
travel on archeological digs in far away places.
Ages 8-12.
Retail: $5.99 each

The Mountain that Burns Within	0-78143-001-1
Treasure of the Hidden Tomb	0-78143-003-8
The Valley of the Giants	0-78143-002-X

Time Twist
by Paul McCusker

The Time Twists series encourages readers to realize
God works in ways we don't always see or understand.
It provides a suspenseful, wholesome alternative to the
horror genre currently popular with preteens.
Ages 10 & up.
Retail: $5.99 each

Sudden Switch   0-74593-611-3
Stranger in the Mist   0-74593-612-1
Memory's Gate   0-74593-613-X